THRILL KILLERS

STEVEN CAUMO

Grindhouse Press #114
ISBN-13: 978-1-957504-29-2

For Dallas Mayr, AKA Jack Ketchum

THE FIRST DAY

TUESDAY, JULY 27th, 2021

12:26 AM

"FOR THE LAST TIME, I said I was sorry."

Paul was drunk. Dead drunk. No surprise there. They'd both been drinking heavily since dinner. This was only their second bar of the night, and Laura was pretty sure they'd be getting kicked out of here too. Paul kept spilling his beer and ogling the two girls a few stools down, oblivious to their matching engagement rings.

So far, their trip to Paradise was a disaster. The drive from Akron to Maryland took over twelve hours because Paul refused to take any toll roads. Laura would be shocked if his battered old Honda Accord survived the trip back. If she'd gotten her way to begin with, they would be enjoying clear blue skies and soaking up golden sunshine in the Bahamas. But of course, Paul "forgot" to fill out his passport application, so here they were in a dingy boardwalk tavern hoping the next tram reached the station before the rain started. Tomorrow's plans for indoor minigolf, arcade games, and what would no doubt be awkward, fumbling, and mutually unsatisfying sex did little to improve her mood.

Laura knew she would forgive him eventually. She always did. She loved him.

The trouble was Laura was drunk too. And she wanted to fight.

"If you were really sorry," Laura said, pausing to sip her gin and tonic. "You wouldn't have said it in the first place."

Paul downed the rest of his Miller Lite and brought the glass down hard on the countertop. The bartender cast a wary look in their direction but didn't approach.

"That doesn't even make any sense! And I meant it as a compliment."

"I thought you said it was a joke."

Earlier, while wandering aimlessly on the boardwalk discussing where to eat that night, they had passed a display of vulgar tee shirts outside one of the countless souvenir shops. Paul had stopped and pointed.

"You should get that one!"

In all caps, the shirt read: WITH A ASS LIKE THIS WHO NEEDS TITS?

Laura flushed with anger and insecurity. Never mind the improper grammar. She was certain that Paul only said something because she had just refused to go to Hooters for dinner that night. She wanted something local. Authentic. She was even abstaining from Starbucks and Dunkin while they were here. Paul never wanted to try new things, except in the bedroom.

"You're impossible," Paul said. He shook his head and sighed, then belched. "We should have just gone back to the room after dinner."

Laura hated to agree, but he was right.

After barely cooling down from the tee shirt incident, they'd gone to a brand-new Italian restaurant for dinner where the manager/owner greeted them at the door, proudly informed them that they would be his first customers. Laura sincerely hoped they would also be his last.

Being understaffed, she could forgive. Her first job was in food service. But the waitress, a surly old hag who might have been the man's wife or mother (or both, Paul suggested) had been rude and impatient, acting personally offended at their valid criticisms: Laura's vodka lemonade was just a tall glass of vodka with a wedge of lemon on top; Paul's chianti looked, smelled, and tasted like cough syrup; the calamari appetizer was too chewy; Laura's "freshly baked" lobster ravioli was still frozen; Paul's requested rare burger was burnt black to the center. Laura had never left a one-star review faster in her life, and for once she didn't admonish Paul for not tipping.

"I told you that dump was a bad idea," Paul said as they left.

"No, you didn't! I said it sounded nice and you just went along like always. If you have a problem, say something. I'm not a mind reader."

He muttered something, walking ahead of her.

"What was that?"

"Nothing."

"I can't hear you when you look away from me and talk at the same time."

"It was nothing! I made a noise is all. Christ. Give me a break already."

After that they barely spoke, their stomachs still growling, both tense and buzzed. Back on the boardwalk they found their way to a tiki bar on 3rd Street outside a much nicer hotel than the one they were staying at, which Laura felt the need to comment on. They spent the next hour trying the patience of the bartender, running the man ragged, ordering new drinks before he could even set down the ones he'd just prepared. When he finally cut them off Laura started an argument when Paul didn't want to tip this time. She ended up slamming down a twenty-dollar bill from her own wallet in a huff, knocking over her stool as she stood, too angry and embarrassed to pick it back up as she stalked out of the bar with Paul right on her heels.

If she'd just gone in the other direction back to the hotel maybe they'd have made up by now. Or at the very least fallen asleep.

Instead, Paul and Laura walked south through a dense mob of sweaty tourists, drunkenly weaving their way around long lines for overpriced ice cream and funnel cake, breaking from the pack only once to use the disgusting and equally crowded public restrooms, where they both stepped in piss. Every so often the constant motion on the boardwalk stopped abruptly as small groups gathered around street performers. A skinny white boy at a karaoke stand sang "Gold Digger" without censoring himself. In front of a row of biblical sand sculptures, a young man preached from Revelations and asked his audience, "If you died today, do you know for a fact that you'd go to heaven?" At the 9/11 memorial, where another man was performing magic tricks, Laura's foot started hurting. She stopped and grabbed Paul's arm for support.

"Get off me!"

He pulled away from her, unable to conceal the disgust on his face. Wobbling on one leg, she took off her left sandal. There was a throbbing blister on her big toe the size of her thumb. Laura wanted Paul to get the car and pick her up at the nearest side street. Not wanting to lose his parking place in the lot across from their hotel, Paul insisted she tough it out and take the tram. They were already close to the end of the boardwalk. It wasn't that far. Laura put her sandal back on and begrudgingly agreed.

They reached the station just as a tram departed, fully loaded with passengers from the amusement park on the pier and blaring its horn at those idling in its path.

"Now what?" Laura asked.

"Calm down. We'll catch the next one. Look, there's another bar right over there. We can have a few more drinks and maybe get some food that's actually edible."

So here they were, losing track of time and more sheets to the wind than Laura cared to count. Looking around at their fellow drinkers at the bar and in the booths, all twenty-somethings probably still in college or freshly graduated, she thought she and Paul must be the oldest people here. Even the bartender was baby-faced. *We don't belong here*, Laura thought. Then, *I don't belong here*.

"What did you say?" Laura asked.

"I didn't say anything."

"Not now. Earlier. After dinner."

"What the hell are you talking about."

"You said you hated me."

"No, I didn't. Keep your voice down."

Laura couldn't help it. She was crying.

"I want to go home," Laura sobbed. She said it again, hitting the counter with her fist for emphasis on every word.

People were staring. The bartender came over and told Paul it was time to pay up and get out. Laura didn't wait. She rushed out of the bar, limping from her bad toe and ignoring Paul's calls for her to slow down and wait. She would get back to the hotel, get the car keys and take off without him. Leave Paul stranded in Maryland. That would show him.

She managed to stumble back to the tram station. All the lights were off. The place was deserted. A "closed" sign hung against the darkened ticket window. They had lost track of time at the bar and missed the last one.

When Paul didn't come running after her, apologizing and

begging for forgiveness, promising to do better and declaring his love, Laura stumbled toward the nearest ramp onto the beach. She kicked off her sandals. They'd been a birthday gift from Paul. Half a size too small. She flung them at a garbage can and missed. Slowly, Laura made her way through the sand to the edge of the shore and sat down.

The tide was low. Before her the Atlantic stretched into the night, an infinite pool of darkness. There were ships on the horizon, their dim pinprick lights paling in comparison to the electric glow of streetlights on the boardwalk now far behind her. She buried her face against her knees, not caring that her shorts were getting wet. She would just stay here until the water swallowed and drowned her like in that Florence + the Machine song.

Laura heard footsteps. They were soft and measured but still barely audible. *Paul?* She turned her head and saw a woman approaching from the shadows on her right.

"Hey," the stranger said. "Are you okay?"

Laura blubbered incoherently, feeling ridiculous and humiliated.

The woman sat down next to her. Half-blinded by tears, Laura could see the woman's blonde hair but little else. When the woman held out tissues from her purse, Laura noticed a wedding ring on her finger. A big one. That just made her cry harder. She took the tissues anyway.

"I saw you leaving the bar," the stranger said. "You seemed pretty upset. Is that jerk you were with your husband?"

Laura shook her head and wiped her face.

"I heard him asking people if there were any other bars in walking distance after you left. I guess you're not a local, huh?"

She shook her head again and blew her nose. The woman kept talking.

"Are you staying nearby? On the boardwalk? In town? With friends? Is there anyone else who might come looking for you tonight?"

What was with all these questions? Laura wanted to be comforted, not interrogated. Was this lady a cop? She tried to blink away the last of her tears, rubbing her eyes with the back of her hands and letting the tissue drop into the sand. When she looked up the woman's face was inches away from her own. Whoever she was, she was beautiful.

And smiling like a lunatic.

"Why don't you come with me? My husband and I have a condo on the north side. Nice and quiet. Soundproofed actually. You can rest. Relax. Maybe even enjoy yourself a little."

Laura felt icy water lapping at her feet. It should have soothed her aching, swollen toe. Instead, it doubled the sobering chill working its way through her body.

"Um, no thank you," Laura said. She tried to stand. "I just needed some space to clear my head. I think I'll—"

She was going to say *Go back to my hotel and wait for my boyfriend* when a hand closed over her mouth from behind. There was a sharp, burning pain as something stung the side of her neck, and then just as quickly Laura felt no pain anywhere at all. She slumped down in the sand.

"Did I do good, baby?" the woman asked.

"You did great, honey," a man's voice replied.

Their hands scooped Laura up under both arms, and then she was being dragged away from the water back toward the boardwalk. Her entire body felt tingly but good. Better than good. Better than she'd ever felt in her entire life. One moment her feet were on the sand, then they were on the boards, and then they were on the sidewalk.

Laura was put into the back seat of a car. It had leather seats. They smelled nice. The woman buckled her in. The car started moving. She closed her eyes.

Eventually the car stopped.

Laura was still conscious but couldn't open her eyes.

Someone unbuckled her. She felt hands carrying her again, heard elevator doors open and close, and then they were going up. When it stopped and they got off Laura was barely breathing. A key card dinged. Another door opened and closed. Locks turned. Where was she? Where was Paul? Why wasn't he here?

"Have fun tonight, baby," the woman said. "You deserve it."

And then the hands began taking off Laura's clothes.

7:09 AM

JACK HOPED HE WAS MAKING the right decision. He checked the time on his microwave, guessed he had a few more minutes, and lit another cigarette off the stovetop burner. Diane didn't like it when he did that. If everything went according to plan though, this might be the last time he could get away with it.

He sat down at the kitchen table, Winston in one hand and a pen in the other. His cup of coffee was cold, but that never stopped him. Bad coffee was better than no coffee. Just like no wine was better than bad wine. Jack clicked his pen, turned the page of his yellow legal pad, and reviewed his packing checklist.

Towels, toothbrush, toiletries? Check.

Shorts, shirts, socks, sandals, sweatshirt, swim trunks? Check.

Engagement ring?

He put the pen down a moment and felt the ring resting in his front right pocket.

Check.

The cats stared at him from the doorway. Scruffy curious. Midnight pouting. They always did this before he went anywhere. Other than work, the last time he'd had to leave them under someone else's care was when he moved back to Pennsylvania last summer.

His house was the one he was raised in, just like his father before him. Jack had known for a long time that inheritance would be his only opportunity for home ownership. Over the last fourteen years he'd worked as a fast-food cashier, shelved books at a library, acted on the stage, been a security guard at a museum by day and tended bar by night while getting his master's degree. Right now, he was selling shoes at the nearby outlet. Next month he would resume teaching high school English. On his days off he made abstract oil paintings and wrote free verse poetry. His guitar was currently gathering dust in a closet. It would have been nice to perform again, but there weren't many venues for folk rock in Evergreen.

Jack checked his other pocket. He knew he'd need to save the rest of the red soft pack for when he was crossing the Bay Bridge. There was something else to go with the ring in there too. Part of the surprise.

Midnight hissed, leaping to the table on his wobbly old legs. Scruffy followed her mate in silence. When Jack found them, he was living in a studio apartment, and they were scavenging in a dumpster. At the time they were probably eating better than he was. In fact, they probably still were. He kissed them once each on the tops of their heads, Midnight trying to push Scruffy out of the way for more attention as usual. Jack laughed, remembering how long it had taken the once vicious tomcat to take his affection. Now the big jerk couldn't get enough of it.

He heard Diane's car pull into the driveway. Jack stubbed out his cigarette and went to collect his bags.

"Now you two be on your best behavior while I'm gone," Jack said. "Dennis will be here later today and stay with you until I come back on Sunday."

His cousin lived just up the road. He was a good kid, reliable, and if he decided to invite any friends over while Jack was away the only rules were that they leave everything the way they found it and respect his cats. Jack abhorred violence but if anyone ever hurt his babies, intentionally or not, he thought he might be capable of anything.

She knocked on the front door even though she had a key. Jack opened it.

"Good morning," Diane said. "Do you have a minute to talk about our Lord and Savior Jesus Christ?"

Jack shut the door in her face. After a beat he opened it again.

Diane walked in laughing, kissed him, and he could have proposed to her right there.

"Sorry. I couldn't resist. You ready?"

"Yep. Do you need to use the bathroom?"

"No."

"Do you mean 'yes'?"

"You know me so well."

She took off her sunglasses and disappeared down the hall. He watched her go, drinking her in. Thick red hair piled on top of her head in a messy bun. Spaghetti strap tank top and cutoff denim shorts that made her look like she just walked off the cover of a Carl Hiaasen novel. Smooth, well-muscled arms and legs from a disciplined workout regimen. Even after two years together it was still hard enough for him to believe that former homecoming queen Diane Prescott was in his house, let alone his girlfriend.

"Are you still okay driving the first hour and a half?" Diane called out.

"Yeah, babe."

According to Google Maps, the trip would take six hours and thirty minutes with no stops. Just over three hundred and seventy-five miles to Paradise, Maryland. Factoring in breakfast, gas, bathroom breaks, traffic, any other spontaneous pit stops they made along the way, and the diversion Jack secretly had planned, it would be at least nine hours on the road before they reached their destination. Check-in time was at four, so that worked out perfectly. He heard the toilet flush and the sound of running water as Diane washed her hands.

She came out of the bathroom and both cats ran to greet her.

"There's my handsome man and pretty lady," Diane said. She picked up Midnight and cradled him in one arm while Scruffy rubbed her face against Diane's legs.

Yes, Jack was making the right decision. He smiled.

They would remember this vacation forever.

8:18 AM

SHE'D OVERSLEPT AND MISSED THE sunrise again, goddammit. Two weeks in this overpriced tourist trap and Claire had yet to so much as glimpse one. This hangover was killing her. She felt deader than the woman Brett was currently fucking. *Better not get any shit on my sheets,* Claire thought. They were a wedding present from her mother worth five thousand dollars. Made in Italy. Maybe she would finally get around to writing thank you cards today.

Yawning, Claire climbed out of the guest bed and pulled on her robe. The best part of sleeping on the first floor was that she didn't need to risk breaking her neck coming down the stairs from the master suite, which was a genuine concern given how intense her hangovers were getting to be. The worst part was not getting to kiss Brett first thing in the morning, even if he did have the nastiest morning breath in the world. It was like a rat crawled in there and died every night.

Upstairs the king size bed kept on squeaking.

She made the short trek into the open concept kitchen and living room. The Keurig needed descaling but that could wait. She was in the mood for caramel vanilla coffee with extra cream and sugar.

When it was ready Claire took it and the Nora Roberts paperback she'd been slogging through for almost a month now onto the first floor's private oceanfront balcony.

Today it was supposed to rain off and on, with a thunderstorm in the forecast tonight. Right now, the sky was overcast and the water looked rough. She recognized the bubbling white foam of a rip current. At least there wouldn't be any squealing brats out in the pool today, but you never knew for sure. Their condo was on the top floor, but the sound of children could still carry up to the balconies from the outdoor pool twelve stories below, but only the balconies. Claire wasn't lying to the woman they grabbed off the beach last night. Every room at the complex was supposed to be thoroughly soundproofed. They only heard their neighbors, a blended family with a sulking teen and squealing toddler, if they were outside. Claire was grateful for the morning silence.

She needed to remember to ditch the woman's driver's license along with the rest of the never-ending list of crap she had to do one of these days. It was in Claire's purse along with the needle they had used to drug the girl with an overdose of heroin. Her cellphone was already smashed to bits. Brett was paranoid about being tracked, but they were so high up and there were so many other units Claire thought he was making a big deal out of nothing. What else was there? Not much. Credit cards and a room key. Their victim traveled light. There'd been some cash in her wallet that Brett would be eager to spend, not that they needed it.

Claire's parents owned a great deal of land and a diverse stock portfolio. She'd gone to college with all tuition paid for a degree in communications, the easiest major she could think of. Not that she ever planned to use it. Claire had never worked a day in her life. But her parents insisted she get an education, which was her mother's way of saying get married. And she'd certainly done that, not that they ever expected her to meet a man like Brett. No one did. Especially not her.

When she was a teenager, she'd planned to seduce one of her father's friends, preferably a doctor who was already married. Maybe start by sleeping with his son, even go as far to get engaged to him. Fucking them both while the younger was completely oblivious and the elder all too aware of the situation, hating every minute of it but unable to resist her. Then staging a nice big car accident for mommy and sonny, leaving poor daddy and Claire helpless but to find comfort in each other's arms.

She blamed growing up watching soap operas for her romantic, overactive imagination. In truth, Claire had thought she would never find true love. Doubted that it even existed.

Then along came Brett.

Her sorority sisters sneered, her mother about had a heart attack, and her father might have killed Brett if Brett weren't two hundred and ten pounds of pure muscle.

The sliding glass door opened behind her. She set the book aside and looked up at her husband. Brett was naked, blood on his mouth, hands, and penis. This high up, there was no chance of anyone seeing him.

"Morning sexy," Claire said.

His sticky hands began rubbing her shoulders. She sighed, not realizing how tight her muscles had been.

"Sleep okay last night?" Brett asked.

"I guess. I missed you."

"Missed you too. How much did you have to drink last night?"

"Just a bottle of prosecco. And whatever I had at the bar before we saw your new toy."

She reached back and gave his balls an affectionate squeeze.

"So, how was it?"

"Baby, it was even better than I ever dreamed. I mean, wow. Dead pussy is something else. It about sucked me dry."

"What about her tits?"

"Eh, I left them alone. I wasn't that hungry."

"It's okay. We're here through Labor Day anyway. You still have plenty of time."

He pointed to her book.

"Making any progress?"

"No. The stupid main character and her boyfriend just keep drinking wine, eating pizza, fucking without a condom and then arguing about the serial killer coming after her. The same crap, over and over. It's insulting. In fact—"

She picked up the novel and threw it over the guardrail. The pages flapped in the wind for a moment and then the book was gone.

Brett laughed. "I love you so much."

"I love you more."

"Nuh-uh."

"Uh-huh. But that does remind me, what do you want for dinner tonight?"

"How about wings?"

"Fine. But no delivery. The trash is already overflowing. I saw a place on the boardwalk last night that looks good."

"Okay. Still want to do brunch at the marina?"

"Absolutely. I could kill for a Bloody Mary right now. My head hurts so bad."

"Aw, poor baby."

He kissed the top of her head.

"You should take a quick nap after you shower," Claire said. "I'll bag up what's left of whatshername. Then I'll get cleaned up and wake you so we can dump her and go straight to brunch."

"Sounds good to me."

"The plastic cover didn't slip, did it?"

"Not an inch."

"Good."

He kissed her again and went inside. Claire took the opportunity to stare at his ass. His tan line was atrocious, but she loved him anyway. She wondered what she would order with her Bloody Mary. Probably something light. She was trying to watch her figure.

The sliding door on the next balcony, fully obscured by a dividing wall, opened and closed. In a minute the stink of a watermelon vape pen filled the air. The neighbor girl was awake, puffing away while her father and stepmother probably continued to doze. It was a disgusting habit, in Claire's opinion. At least smoking cigarettes looked cool.

Her mind wandered from brunch to how she might get the girl over here one afternoon without her parents knowing, and all the different ways she and Brett could make her scream, her family next door all the while without the faintest idea.

11:40 AM

DIANE THOUGHT THEY WERE MAKING good time on the drive. They had traveled south then east through West Virginia to avoid toll roads. They passed lush, rolling hills clustered with trees along the winding highway. It was beautiful, but still, they paled in comparison to the mountains she had seen and climbed out west. Diane had flown across the country more times than she could count, but she preferred traveling by car whenever possible. Driving gave her a sense of control. Today though, she didn't mind being a passenger, especially in her cherry red Ford Mustang convertible with the top down and her boyfriend at the wheel.

They made it into Maryland at a quarter to nine and stopped at an IHOP just over the border for breakfast. She and Jack both needed to be up and running for a few hours before they could develop an appetite, and Diane had been awake since before five to exercise. It was a habit she developed during her days as a client service consultant for an investment bank. Amidst the drudgery of constant travel, soul sucking meetings, and complimentary hotel breakfasts that ranged from abysmal to mediocre, even just thirty minutes on an elliptical or treadmill each morning kept her sane. Now that she had a desk job as director of quality and performance improvement for a nonprofit, she ate better, stressed less, and exercised at the same gym six days a week. Of course, if it weren't for that bank job, she may never have reconnected with Jack.

Diane didn't believe in fate. She believed in numbers and data, although she acknowledged luck as an influential if volatile market factor. The probability of them running into each other ten years since their high school graduation and in a different state must have been absurdly low. Even on his drunkest day Bukowski wouldn't have bet on those odds. But it happened, and now Jack McKee's middle school wet dreams were a reality. Watching him stuff his face with country fried steak and hashbrowns, Diane wondered what her teenage self would find harder to believe: that the skinny dork everyone used to call Nips fucked her brains out on a regular basis, or that at thirty she was happier and healthier than she'd ever been in her life.

After they finished their meal and stocked up on a few car snacks at the adjoining BFS station, Diane took over for the next leg of the drive.

"What do you want to listen to next?" Jack asked. They had already worked their way through ZZ Top's Greatest Hits album.

She gave him a mischievous look.

"You know what."

Jack rolled his eyes but couldn't help grinning as he queued up her playlist. For the next four minutes and sixteen seconds, John Mellencamp sang their song, and although Diane had her share of fun in the backseat of his car, her Jack was about the furthest thing from a football star you could get. Next was "Mustang Sally," followed by Jefferson Airplane, Bruce Springsteen, Tracy Chapman, and so on. What Jack lovingly referred to as her divorced dad rock music went on for another hour and a half before they stopped for gas and a bathroom break.

Diane stood by the car while Jack went inside to piss and probably bought more cigarettes. It was funny. She'd always hated the stink of them, but ever since they started dating, she found their aroma comforting. Whenever Jack spent the night at her apartment, after he left, she would greedily sniff his pillow. Still, she hoped he'd quit sooner rather than later. For the first time since Andrea, she actually pictured spending her life with someone.

Don't, Diane scolded herself. *Don't think about her. Not now.*

Every so often her ex-girlfriend wormed her way into her

thoughts. Diane would be at the grocery store, working late at the office, getting coffee. Completely focused on the task at hand. Then the wondering would start. What was Andrea eating for dinner that night? Would Andrea think the video she just watched was funny? Where was Andrea right now and was she thinking about her too?

It was stupid. The last thing Diane wanted to do was let Andrea spoil things between her and Jack when Andrea probably hadn't thought about her since their breakup. Jack knew all about her of course. He had his share of bisexual encounters, kissing more men than she had, in fact, the most serious of which was during college with his closeted junior year RA. But that was casual, like most of his relationships before Diane. What she and Andrea had was serious. Intense. And toxic.

She'd taken that godawful consulting job in the first place for Andrea, who never bothered to finish her performing arts degree and just couldn't seem to find employment anywhere. Diane practically worked herself to death to pay for the expensive Philadelphia townhouse they rented together while Andrea didn't cook or clean or do much of anything except—as Diane later found out—sleep with exboyfriends when Diane was out of town. The last she heard, Andrea married one of them. They even had a baby. Just about everyone she and Jack went to high school with had babies now. There was a new Facebook announcement every week. It wasn't something Diane had ever wanted, and an ectopic miscarriage her freshman year of college rendered any chance of changing her mind one day moot.

Diane was drowning her sorrows about Andrea's marriage at a dive bar in Kent, Ohio, a walk down the street from her hotel when Jack, a regular, sat down next to her. They'd looked at each other, done a double take, and then that was that. They were an item by closing time.

She was in love with Jack. Wanted to spend the rest of her life with him. But every so often that old wound opened inside her heart and with it came fear. The fear she wasn't good enough. That she tried her hardest before and in the end none of it mattered. She had failed once and she would fail again.

Jack emerged from the gas station carrying a plastic bag.

"Found you a present."

He presented her with a Coke bottle with her name on it, then produced one with his own.

"Had to dig back in the cooler to find them both. And that's not all."

Next came a chocolate Payday bar, something Diane had been obsessed with since reading *The Stand* during lockdown last summer. It was a simple gesture, but with it the dark cloud that had gathered so quickly in his absence faded completely. Jack had that effect on her. From the way she smiled at him, someone walking by might have thought he was giving her a diamond.

11:59 AM

BRETT SQUEEZED A SLICE OF lemon onto the oyster, applied a generous amount of cocktail and horseradish sauce using the little two-pronged fork that came with the order, then slurped it down and belched. He was really starting to like the slimy little guys. Until he came to Maryland, he never understood their appeal. Never mind the adage that they were an aphrodisiac. Brett never liked admitting when he was wrong, but on this he was willing to concede. Just ask the bitch whose body they dumped an hour ago. He'd played with the pieces all night long. If Brett had to pick a favorite, he'd have to go with her head. The bottom though, not the mouth. It was in a garbage bag in a Delaware landfill now along with the rest of her.

He and Claire were seated outside the restaurant. The sky still looked shitty, but the ocean was a nice shade of indigo. Docked boats bobbed along the pier. Brett loved to look at them. He'd grown up in landlocked Illinois, mostly in and around Galesburg. Never went to the beach until he was twenty, not long after his first tour with the Air Force. That was in North Carolina. He didn't spend much time there before being transferred to Ohio. This was before his dishonorable discharge. Before he met Claire. Back when he was just an average rapist.

She had shown him he could be so much more.

Brett watched Claire sip her Bloody Mary. He thought her sunglasses made her look like a movie star. Never mind the clouds overhead. The ice tinkled in her glass and the various garnishes twirled in the thick red liquid. At least he knew she would eat those. Anything soaked in vodka was always a safe bet. There was a bacon strip, celery stalk, and olives on a toothpick, plus lime and lemon wedges. Probably a third of a day's calories total.

"You sure you don't want one, babe?" Brett asked, holding out the last mollusk.

"No thank you," Claire said. "I don't want to spoil my appetite."

Brett frowned. He'd noticed Claire was eating less and drinking more since they arrived in the bustling beach town. It scared him. And the fact that he felt any concern for anyone but himself also scared him. In fact, until he met Claire, he never felt much of anything except hunger, tiredness, and The Urge.

The Urge began during puberty and had been with him ever since.

He was at the reserve station in Vienna, not too far from Youngstown, spending whatever free time he had scoping out the campus for potential prey to satisfy The Urge. Brett saw her immediately. Turned out she'd seen him too. Brett still got chills when he remembered waiting outside of her sorority house that night, making sure the rest of them were out, creeping up to a window near the back when her voice called out to him.

"The front door's unlocked."

He could have turned and ran right there. He almost did. He wanted to. Instead, he marched up to the front door and walked right in.

"I'm in the kitchen."

Brett thought he must have been dreaming. She was standing there completely naked except for an apron, cooking him dinner.

"Five more minutes. Have a seat. My name's Claire. What's yours?"

And before he knew it, he was sitting down and telling her his actual name, where he worked, where he was from. His entire goddamn life story. Divorced parents. The Air Force. The rapes. She was especially interested in the rapes.

"Have you ever killed anyone before?" Claire asked.

No, he hadn't., Came close a couple of times but never went all the way. She climbed into his lap, pulled off his ski mask, and smiled at him.

"I have."

The waitress appeared, snapping Brett out of his remembrance. She set the large steamer pot down for him and a plate of crab and avocado toast with fresh tomato slices on the side for Claire. That she had carried both balanced on one tray impressed him.

"Anything else I can get you two?" she asked. "Another drink?"

Claire said yes and Brett said no, even though his Heineken was almost empty and she still had half of her Bloody Mary left. Brett said what the hell and asked for another. They had walked to the dockside pub from their condo anyway. His market price meal meant for two included snow crab legs, mussels, clams, shrimp, coleslaw, and corn on the cob. He stared at the waitress as she walked away, thinking about how much nicer it would have been to have her in bed last night instead of the tourist.

Claire read his mind.

"Don't worry B. The next one will be better."

"I know." He cracked open a crab leg with his hands and sucked the sweet white meat straight out. Through a mouthful of carrion eater, he said, "First, we need to find you a friend for tonight. Any ideas?"

"Actually, yes."

She chugged the rest of her Bloody Mary, licked off the salt and pepper rim. The sight of her tongue against the glass made him hard. Claire popped a plump green olive into her mouth and chewed thoughtfully.

"Do you know how many foreign students are working in Paradise this summer?"

Brett shrugged. "I don't know. A hundred?"

"Try a thousand. Normally it's more like four or five thousand, but everyone's still cagey after the pandemic."

"That's understandable."

"Tell that to my mother. She called me while you were resting earlier. Wants to know when a good weekend would be for her and Daddy to make the drive from Bel Air to come visit. Then she asked if I got 'the jab' for about the billionth time."

"And did you lie and say no for the billionth time?"

"Duh. She'd disinherit me if I didn't."

"Good thing you've had years of practice."

"Amen."

He drank the rest of his beer, and they clinked their empty glasses together. It was something they did every morning whether they ate out or at home. After their first night together, they'd gone to a Waffle House for breakfast. Without really thinking about it they'd toasted their newfound arrangement with their coffee mugs. An old woman at the next table looked over at them and smiled, told them she and her husband did the same thing every morning for fifty years. Brett and Claire had looked across the table at each other, both imagining all they might accomplish together. Brett grinned. Dreams really did come true.

3:25 PM

THEY WERE ABOUT TWENTY MINUTES away from their hotel when Jack took a blindfold out of his pocket and asked her to put it on.

"Ooh, is this a new way to play highway hand job?" Diane asked.

"No," Jack said. "This is better."

She tied the black velvet around her eyes without complaint.

"You *sure* you don't want another highway hand job?"

"I'm sure. And that was one time. You're never going to let it go, are you?"

"Nope."

Diane was excited. Not just for whatever surprise Jack had in mind, but to finally see Paradise. For all her traveling, she'd never been. Growing up, her parents took her to Disney World a few times. Before they lost the farm. Toward the end of their marriage Diane came to dread rather than anticipate those long, sweltering car rides to Florida. But Jack's mother and father always took him to Paradise when they could afford it. There were actual photo albums and home video tapes documenting his growth from chubby blond toddler to lanky dark-haired teen on that beach and boardwalk.

They'd crossed the Bay Bridge about two hours ago. Jack kept both hands on the wheel and a cigarette in his mouth for the whole four miles. Diane was as in awe of the impressive metal work as she was the gorgeous view of the water. After avoiding the Baltimore Beltway and DC traffic, the rest of the drive was a straight shot to their destination. They'd made one last pit stop at a produce stand. There was a wicker basket loaded up with peaches and cantaloupe in their backseat. Diane wanted to stop there again on their way back. There was a used bookstore they passed she was interested in visiting on their way back as well. It was supposed to be her turn to drive again, but Jack insisted on getting back behind the wheel.

Now she knew why.

Diane heard the top going up. In another minute the light pitter patter of rain on the windshield and the mechanical whir of the wiper blades on their lowest setting began. The car turned right. Jack had changed and muted the directions on the GPS.

"Do you want to listen to any music?" Jack asked.

Diane shook her head. Where could they be? She tried to remember what else was in the general area. A few small towns. A lot of motels. And something else. A National Park maybe? She heard Jack muttering about the weather. He seemed tense. Like he was second guessing himself. She reached over and put her hand on his knee, felt him relax at her touch.

"I love you," Diane said.

"Love you too."

The car slowed and turned again. The sound of rain became muted. Blocked out by tree branches overhead maybe? She thought her guess about the National Park was spot on. What could they be doing here?

Jack parked and told her to keep the blindfold on just a little longer. He helped her out of her seat and locked the car. He took her hand and began leading her somewhere.

"Watch your step. Careful."

They were on a sandy trail. The rain had stopped for now. Diane smelled the heavy salt air. And something else. Something she hadn't smelled in years.

"Jack, where—"

"Just a moment. Wait right here."

She felt his hand slip out of her grasp and heard his footsteps moving away further into the unknown. Her heart began to race but not with fear. This was something else. Diane didn't know what, but she knew something was happening. Something important.

Jack's footsteps returned.

"Okay, just a little further."

He wrapped an arm around her shoulder, guiding her in a new direction. The familiar scent grew stronger, warm and earthy, almost stronger than the sea itself. A minute later, Jack moved behind her and untied the blindfold.

She was staring at a dozen horses fifty feet away. There were foals playing at the edge of the water while a group of mares kept watch at a reasonable distance. Further up the shore, two stallions were rough housing. She could see their powerful muscles working under their red and white manes. These were wild horses. She'd read about them and forgotten. Great big beasts that roamed the coast of this little island, living their whole lives free to do as they pleased.

"They're beautiful," Diane said.

There were tears in her eyes. She turned and Jack was no longer standing.

He was down on one knee.

In his hand, a garnet ring glimmered.

"Diane—"

"Yes."

"—will—"

"Yes!"

"—you—"

She was on him before he could finish, kissing his face and neck. They rolled in the sand, Jack struggling not to drop the ring. Down they went, laughing, both happier than they'd ever been before. Diane felt something wet beneath her as they came to a stop, and an even stronger smell assaulted her nostrils. Another one from a lifetime ago. It was unmistakable.

Jack's nose scrunched up. He looked down at what they were lying in.

"Oh God. Is this—?"

"It sure is."

Both of their shirts were smeared with horse shit.

"Please tell me this is good luck," Jack said.

"The best," Diane said, and kissed him again.

4:04 PM

THE WOMAN AT THE FRONT desk had the courtesy not to comment on their pungent odor or the dark stains on their outfits. Thankfully Jack and Diane only needed one trip to get their luggage up to the room, so stares from other guests were kept to a minimum. He'd dug out two of their beach towels to cover the car seats, not that Diane noticed. When she wasn't looking at her ring, she was looking at him, and he knew better than anyone how she intended to celebrate. But first they needed to shower.

Their room had an oceanfront view, currently obscured by a steady downpour. They stripped and bundled their soiled and sweaty clothes into one of the white garbage bags they'd brought with them for dirty laundry.

In the bathroom Diane unpacked their toiletries while Jack got the shower going nice and hot. Steam filled the air. She let her hair down and looked in the mirror, carefully examining her ginger locks, visibly relieved they had escaped the roll in the dirt unscathed. Jack came up behind her, pressing his erection into the small of her back.

"You ready?" he asked.

Diane reached around, felt the tip of his glans poking out of his foreskin.

"You know I am."

They washed first. Jack moved his fingers delicately on her scalp, easing the knots out of her hair just as tenderly as he always rubbed her clitoris. When he lathered her breasts with soap he moved her nipples clockwise, and when he rinsed them, he moved them counterclockwise. Diane bit her bottom lip.

"I can't wait," she said. "I want it here."

"You don't want me to go down on you first?"

"Later. I need you now."

She turned to face him, wrapping her arms around his neck for support as she raised her left leg. Jack lifted her up and entered her with ease. Diane locked her legs around his waist and moaned as he pressed her back against the tile wall, both of his calloused hands firm on her ass.

But Jack wasn't satisfied with just thrusting. He was going to use his mouth to please her one way or another. He sucked on her left nipple until she was clawing his back and then on her right until she was moaning his name. This was always his signal for the grand finale. He straightened his back and adjusted his hold on her, pressed his forehead against hers so there was nowhere for either of them to look except into each other's eyes, hers delirious with pleasure and his set in determination to make her come.

"Jack," she whimpered. "I love you, Jack. I love—"

Her scream was involuntary, abrupt and guttural as her entire body shook with orgasm. Jack came deep inside her and held her pressed between his body and the wall.

They tightened their grip on one another and stayed like that awhile, catching their breath as water continued to wash over them until he softened and slipped out of her. Carefully, Jack stepped back as Diane put her feet on the floor of the tub. He didn't let go until he was sure she could stand unsupported. She held onto him for a little while longer anyway.

6:00 PM

JACK AND DIANE MADE THEIR way to a well-reviewed bar and grill on 2nd Street. The rain did not leave the boardwalk completely deserted, and like most of their fellow travelers they carried an umbrella and wore ponchos over their jeans and sweatshirts. Despite the chill they were both warm and content, still flushed from their lovemaking.

At the restaurant, they kept their orders simple. Both had broiled crab cakes on brioche buns, house made potato salad, and Dewar's scotch on the rocks. The food was delicious. Diane thought the potato salad might be the best she'd ever eaten, with thick chunks and a perfect blend of mayo and seasonings.

To their amusement, their waiter was drunk. Diane pegged his accent as Eastern European, which made his uncanny resemblance to a young Dolph Lundgren even more amusing. He had blond hair, blue eyes, and enough muscles bulging under his tight uniform to single-handedly end the Cold War.

"You want to invite him back to our room?" Jack asked. "Make ourselves the bread in a Drago sandwich?"

Diane shushed him when their waiter returned with the check.

Slurred speech aside, he was nice enough. Said he was from Poland and studying to be an airplane mechanic. They tipped him well and kept their table clean.

On their way out, they held the door open for another couple who were coming in from the rain. The words "Thank you" and "You're welcome" were exchanged, but neither pair got a good look at the other. The pleasantries were automatic. Jack and Diane were focused on getting through the rain and back to their room for round two.

Meanwhile, Brett and Claire had just laid eyes on the handsome waiter, who was starting to sober up. He seated them at the very table Jack and Diane occupied just a minute prior.

10:43 PM

PIOTREK COULDN'T BELIEVE HIS LUCK. That morning, he woke up in his tiny roach infested apartment along with seven other young men who spoke a dozen languages between them. He had prepared himself for another long day spent waiting hand and foot on more ungrateful Americans and their rowdy brats, dreaming of a day off to swim in the ocean, soak up some sun, and maybe finally sleep with Hee-jin, the cute Korean girl from down the hall. There had been a lull at work when the rain started earlier that evening, and Piotrek and some of the other guys swiped a bottle of Stoli from behind the bar and passed it around in the kitchen, drinking straight from the bottle. His second-to-last customers were nice enough, leaving behind more cash than anyone else had for him all summer. He chose to take it as a sign of good things to come. And it looked like he was right.

The couple who came in next asked him outright if he'd like to come back to their place after his shift and fuck the wife when he delivered a bread bowl of crab dip to their table. Piotrek took one look at her and said yes. Now he was humping away as she wiggled and squirmed beneath him. Piotrek tried to focus on her breasts and forget he was being watched. The husband was sitting in a chair positioned at the foot of the bed, his eyes locked on Piotrek's impressive glutes. He'd taken off his belt but wasn't even jacking off. Just watching.

Piotrek had read online about guys who got off on this sort of thing. Cucks who enjoyed seeing their women screw other men. Something about humiliation or voyeurism or both turned them on. Personally, he didn't understand the appeal. Not that he was going to complain. But if the husband tried anything gay, Piotrek might have to hurt him. This American was in much better shape than most of the others, but still not as good as Piotrek.

Beneath him the woman pretended to struggle harder. He took hold of her scrawny arms and pinned them roughly above her head. When they started, she had asked him to hurt her. Act like he was forcing himself on her. Do degrading things like spit in her mouth and call her names. Again, Piotrek was not into that sort of thing. He just wanted to bust his nut and call it a night whether he was welcome to sleep over or not. If the half-hearted insults he managed were insufficient, neither of his hosts felt the need to comment on his apparent lack of enthusiasm for roleplaying. Maybe they were as new to this as he was.

He felt himself getting close now. It always took him longer when he wore a condom, but he wasn't going to stick his dick in crazy—no matter how good she looked—without protection. The last thing he needed was an STD in a country with such substandard healthcare. Piotrek's thrusts grew more frantic, building momentum as he stared harder at her tits rocking back and forth. She must have sensed his impending orgasm from the look on his face.

"Stop!" the woman said. "Don't! Please!"

Piotrek figured this was the part where he was supposed to say, "Shut up, bitch" and smack her around a little. Or maybe she wanted him to pull out and let loose on her face. He didn't want to play anymore. Something about her bothered him. Not just the falseness in her voice. It was the look in her eyes. They were aimed over his shoulder, toward her husband.

Piotrek turned his head just as something looped around his throat.

He was jerked backward out of her. She lunged after him as her husband pinned him down. The woman grabbed hold of Piotrek's penis and forced it back inside of her. On top now, she rode him as her husband pressed his belt against Piotrek's throat. The woman threw her head back and moaned. Piotrek struggled to loop his fingers under the taut leather, but the husband had more leverage. He was standing over him now.

"How does it feel, baby?" the man asked.

"Good!" the woman said. "It feels so good! Kiss me."

He obliged, and Piotrek lay there between them as they both leaned forward, tongues in each other's mouths, the husband not letting up on choking him and the wife, if anything, fucking him harder. His hands flailed uselessly at his sides as the world grew darker and the pressure built, not just in his throat and his lungs but in his balls, and then he was coming and despite the pain, despite the terror, despite the blackness about to swallow him whole, it was the strongest orgasm of his life, bursting out of him, breaking the condom from the sheer amount pouring out and he knew he was dying and would never see Hee-jin from down the hall or his awful crowded apartment or Poland and his parents and brothers ever again.

Then just as suddenly as the assault had started, he could breathe again. The man released his grip. The woman dismounted and stood up. Piotrek rolled off the bed and fell to the floor, coughing and shaking as oxygen flooded back into him.

"Son of a bitch!" the woman screamed. She was spreading her labia with her fingers. A glob of his seed oozed out and dripped down her thigh. "The condom broke!"

"Don't worry, babe," her husband said. "We'll get you some Plan B. I think there's still some spermicide in the bathroom anyway."

"Son of a bitch," she said again.

Piotrek heard her storm over to one of the nightstands, opening and then slamming the drawer shut. His sight returned slowly. Black dots and floaters clouded his vision. He spat a thick wad of phlegm onto the hardwood floor.

"Crazy bitch," Piotrek said in Polish. "Fucking psychopaths!"

"What did you say?" the husband asked. "Huh? What did you say, you pinko commie bastard?"

"Fuck you!" Piotrek said in perfect English. He sat up on his knees, ready to spit in the brutish American's face, to kill him and his whore wife with his own two hands.

A gun barrel stared back at him.

"Know what this is?" the woman asked.

Slowly, Piotrek nodded.

"Tell me."

"A g-gun."

"What kind of gun?"

"I-I don't know. P-please—"

"This is my husband's Desert Eagle. I bought it as a birthday present for him last year. It's a .357 Magnum. Know what that means?"

Piotrek began to say the Lord's Prayer in his native tongue for the first time in years. The words came out automatically. Once he started, he couldn't stop. The woman talked over him.

"It means that normally one shot and you're guaranteed dead. But this little cutie has a silencer on it. Makes it nice and quiet but slows the bullet's speed. I could pull the trigger against your skull and there's just the slightest chance it won't kill you. Just hurt you really bad."

She pressed the barrel to his forehead.

"Are you scared? I bet you are. But I promise, if this doesn't kill you, you'll wish it had."

Piotrek was screaming now, reciting the Hail Mary. He was halfway through his third go of it when the woman shoved the gun into his opened mouth, chipping his teeth, pushing it all the way back until it scraped against his uvula. He gagged, still trying to pray, vaguely aware he was pissing all over the floor when the woman pulled the trigger.

Nothing happened.

Piotrek stopped praying.

"You better be ready to clean that up," the woman said, referring to the puddle of urine he was now kneeling in. "Every last drop. I hope you're thirsty."

The woman laughed. She took the gun out of his mouth and brought it down across his face. Piotrek vomited, blood pouring from his broken nose and the woman laughed even harder. She hit him again. And again. And again.

Her husband watched, smiling and smacking his folded belt against his leg, waiting patiently to use it again.

The night was just getting started.

THE SECOND DAY

WEDNESDAY, JULY 28th, 2021

5:58 AM

JACK WAS AWAKE WHEN DIANE got back from the hotel fitness center. It was almost unnecessary after the workout he'd given her last night after dinner, but if she wanted to keep up that kind of pace for the rest of their trip, she needed to stay limber.

She joined him on the balcony. There were two deck chairs and an end table. Judging by his ash tray, Jack hadn't been up long. He took a long drag on what must have been his first cigarette of the day and smiled at her.

"I think I slept twelve hours last night," Jack said.

"That drive really took a lot out of you."

He laughed and stubbed out his Winston. "Yeah, the drive. I'm glad you made it in time. Look over there."

Jack pointed at the ocean. There were still a few clouds lingering, but in a minute the sun broke over the edge of the water. It burned the brightest shade of orange Diane had ever seen, turning the horizon purple. She counted three dolphins gliding through the gentle waves.

"It's beautiful," Diane said.

Jack nodded. "My dad used to wake me up to watch the sunrise whenever we came here. Sometimes when I'm really feeling down, about work, about life, I have a dream that I'm down there on the boardwalk. I'm lucid every time, and the sky always looks just like that. I can smell the air. Taste the salt. I just breathe it all in and walk around until the dream ends."

Diane climbed out of her chair and into his lap.

"What do you want to do today?" Diane asked. "Besides me."

Jack's hands found their way down the back of her yoga pants.

"Bike rentals open at 6:30," he said. "I figured we could ride up and down the boardwalk, go out to the end of the pier. Enjoy the view. Take our time. Come back to the hotel for breakfast, then just spend the morning at the beach. Work on our tans, go swimming. Come back to the room around noon. Shower. Nap. Fuck."

"I like the sound of that. But we still have half an hour to kill."

"I can make coffee. Or go down on you. Or both."

"I'm gross and sweaty."

"I like it when you're gross and sweaty."

"You're such a pervert."

"Well, you are what you eat."

Diane tweaked Jack's nipples through his shirt as he carried her back into the room. He laid her on the bed, then started the coffee. When he came back over, she was already getting started without him. By the time they finished, the coffee was burned, and the best bikes had already been rented. Neither of them minded.

12:15 PM

CLAIRE NEEDED TO HURRY. ***THE*** *Young and the Restless* started soon.

"Come on already."

The number on the meat thermometer slowly rose, point by point, then stopped at 159.

"Damn it!"

She shoved the pan back into the oven and had to restrain herself from slamming it shut. Brett was asleep in the guest room. This was supposed to be a surprise. A reward for all his hard work and support. She didn't need to give him food poisoning from an undercooked lunch. Five more minutes should do the trick. Claire told herself to breathe. Be patient. Patience was one of her few virtues.

After all, she waited until she was sixteen to kill her little brother. God knew that had taken years of restraint. Claire wanted to kill the twerp more times than she could count, but the wait was worth it. She led him out into the woods and took her time with him. No one ever found the body. Officially he was only missing. Every Christmas and on his birthday her parents still held out hope their precious baby boy would come home one day. It grated on her nerves, but there was nothing she could do about it short of confessing. Like that would ever happen.

Her second kill was admittedly more impulsive, and though it all worked out in the end she regretted not getting to savor it. That first semester at Youngstown State she nearly failed Writing 1, and the last thing she needed was a blemish on her transcripts for mommy and daddy to nag her about, let alone the humiliation. Writing 1, for Christ's sake! She had no choice but to leave her roommate hanging from a rope in their closet. Claire worked harder on forging that suicide note than she did on any essay before or after. Everyone bought it, and campus policy guaranteed her all "A"s for her emotional suffering.

Claire counted off on her fingers. The Polish waiter brought her body count to three. She and Brett were tied now. Two boys and a girl for her. Two girls and a boy for him. It would probably do them well to lay off for a while. A week at most. She'd checked the Paradise City Dispatch that morning. The boyfriend of the woman from two nights ago had finally reported her missing. Based on the brief article it looked like the cops figured him for it. Served him right, the jerk. Which reminded her, she still needed to read *Gone Girl.* It had been sitting on her bookshelf far too long. Nothing in the paper about the waiter yet. She doubted there would be. They'd picked their victims well so far.

Still, whoever they did next would have to be special. Something different. The last thing they wanted was to repeat themselves. Routine was the death of romance.

It really was too bad they couldn't kill the assholes next door. After lunch yesterday and before they picked up the waiter, she and Brett ran into them in the lobby. They'd made small talk in the hallways a few times before, and Claire almost immediately decided she disliked them. So of course, the ditzy second wife thought they were best friends. Her name was Janine and her screaming stinking brat was named Adam, who at two would not remember a single moment of this trip despite his mother's insistence about how special everything was.

She was always trying to show Claire pictures on her phone of his first dip in the pool, his first time on the boardwalk, and probably his first shit in the training toilet too. Claire only half-paid attention, deflecting the constant reminders to add or friend or follow Janine with blatant lies about taking a mental health break from social media.

Brett didn't fare much better with Janine's husband, Dan, who was originally from London. He was under the impression Brett's name was Bart and seemed to communicate mostly in *Simpsons* references. The only one of them that remotely interested Claire in the slightest was Violet, the moody scowling teen who never said a word, just seethed and texted in the background. What she gleaned about the girl's life from her father and stepmother was deliciously messy. Apparently, Dan and his first wife used to stay here every year, until she ran off with Violet's eighth grade science teacher, Mr. George. This was his and Violet's first time back here since the divorce. He was either oblivious or in denial about her obvious displeasure.

The idea of taking Violet as a pet, training and breaking her down into complete servitude, crossed Claire's mind more than once. It would be beyond risky, but she would do anything to make Brett happy. Plus, she wouldn't mind having a maid she wouldn't have to pay.

Claire looked around the kitchen for anything else she might do to help pass the time. The sink was packed with crusted over dishes and murky glasses. What didn't fit was littering the counter tops. And the trash still hadn't been taken out. Claire opened one of the cabinets, took out an aerosol spray can of air freshener and gave the room a good spritz. She neglected to put it back afterward.

The guest room door opened. Brett walked in looking perplexed.

"Babe, how come you let me sleep in so late? Now we're not going to be able to get him out of the apartment and clean up until tomorrow."

"It's fine, we can use the other bathroom for another day. Sit down. It's almost ready."

"What's almost ready?"

"Lunch! We've been eating out every day since we got here, so I wanted to surprise you with a homecooked meal."

Brett's face lit up. "Pork chops?" he asked. They were his favorite.

"Almost."

She opened the stove and checked it again. This time it was well over 165. With effort Claire set the heavy metal tray on top of the grimy, grease-stained electric stovetop. The juices popped and sizzled. Brett actually moaned.

"That smells *amazing*."

"I used DoorDash for most of the ingredients," Claire explained. The thought of doing her own grocery shopping was appalling.

"Except for the meat of course."

Sitting amidst Brussel sprouts and diced squash tossed in honey and olive oil was a thick, garlic and herb-encrusted hunk of bone-in human thigh. No fat. Just lean, tender muscles.

"We have to let it sit for ten minutes before we cut it so it doesn't dry out."

He reached around her and tore off a small piece, then moaned again as he chewed.

"You're an artist C. A culinary goddess. Is there anything you can't do?"

Claire giggled and swatted his hand away when he went for another taste. Then she took his wrist and guided that same hand between her legs, his fingers still stained with brown sauce, knowing she could get off and have lunch served before the opening credits rolled.

2:53 PM

DIANE HAD THE STRANGEST DREAM. After a morning spent laughing as they did their best to navigate a tandem bicycle, they'd done as planned and spent nearly five hours on the beach, where she devoured a short horror novel called *Come Closer* that a friend had recommended to her. Either the book or the vinegar-soaked French fries she and Jack shared for lunch was responsible for her troubled sleep.

In the dream she was standing on their hotel balcony. Jack was up to his neck in the water far below her. He waved and said something, but she couldn't hear him. He was too far away. She looked around, saw his lighter, and threw it toward him. Immediately the ocean surged backward and disappeared, leaving behind a moist desert and no sign of Jack. Suddenly transported down to the sand, Diane ran and called his name. She heard the roar of an approaching wave but couldn't see it. The sun was too bright. Diane turned around and the hotel was gone. There was nothing but sand. She ran in slow motion and woke as a tidal wave broke over her back.

Jack was sitting next to her on the bed, stroking the top of her head.

"Hey, it's okay. I'm here. You awake?"

Diane mumbled. He handed her a bottle of Fiji water, which she chugged gratefully. When it was empty she said, "Bad dream."

"I know. You were shaking and kept saying 'no' over and over."

"Really?"

To her knowledge, Diane had never talked in her sleep before.

"Want to talk about it?" Jack asked.

"Not right now. Just hold me a while, okay?"

They snuggled. The thin white sheets felt cool against her bare skin. Jack had the television on with the volume muted. An old episode of 1966 *Batman* was on. Eartha Kitt's Catwoman had the Caped Crusader and Boy Wonder tied up at the mercy of a giant percolator. It ended with a cliffhanger to be continued. Diane guessed part two would start with their escape.

"You want to know something weird?" Jack asked during the commercial break. "There's an episode where they're climbing up the side of a building like they always do. One of the windows opens and Colonel Klink pokes his head out."

Diane thought for a moment. "You mean the bald Nazi from *Hogan's Heroes*?"

"Yeah. Same character, not just the actor."

"That is weird. Does Batman punch him out?"

"No, they just talk to him and make jokes then move along."

"I'd punch him," Diane said. "Break his stupid monocle, pull him out and let him drop."

Jack kissed her neck. "I know you would."

Diane turned away and got to her knees, letting the sheets fall away. She looked over her shoulder. Jack understood immediately. He positioned himself behind her, his hands firm but gentle on her hips. When the show resumed neither of them could be bothered to keep watching.

7:44 PM

"WHERE DO YOU WANT TO go for dinner?"

It was late, but after their afternoon tryst, they'd fallen asleep again, dozing until around six. *We're definitely on vacation time*, Jack thought. They'd watched *Blind Fury* and given their brains even more time to rest.

"There's a place in town I'd like to try," Diane said. She showed him the menu on her phone and Jack scrolled through the options.

"Looks pretty good. Want me to be designated driver?"

"We're on vacation. We should both be able to have fun."

"I don't doubt that we could walk there but depending how much we drink I don't trust myself to make it back here in one piece. It's fifty minutes away on foot."

Diane rolled her eyes.

"Jack. Baby. Light of my life. We can just use a rideshare app."

Jack felt embarrassed at his own naivety. He could be such a country bumpkin sometimes. A few minutes later they were waiting in front of their hotel, facing the city and watching the bumper-to-bumper traffic slowly inch by. Other tourists, even families with small children, ignored the crosswalk and took their chances jaywalking.

"What are we looking for again?" Jack asked.

"A silver Toyota Highlander."

"I don't know what that means."

"It's a big SUV that can seat like six or seven people."

"Isn't that a lot for just the two of us?"

"I picked the carpooling option because it said it would get here faster." Diane checked her phone. "Looks like they just picked somebody else up before us. Is that okay? I can cancel and book another."

Jack shrugged. "I don't mind."

In a few minutes, a car pulled up to the curb. The driver rolled the passenger window and leaned toward them. "Diane Prescott and one guest?" he asked.

Jack and Diane opened the back set of doors and saw the middle two seats were open. The other two passengers were in the back, holding hands.

Once Jack and Diane were buckled up their driver, a big bald man with a thick Yorkshire accent named Tim, rejoined traffic at a steady pace. The air conditioning was at full blast. On the radio they could just barely hear "Sweet Dreams" by Beyonce. Tim quietly sang along and drummed on the steering wheel. They looked back at their fellow travelers and exchanged conspiratorial smiles.

"You guys going to dinner on 49th too?" the man asked. He was handsome in a rough, primitive sort of way, with big muscles. His shoulders were especially huge. They made his bullet shaped head look small on his thick neck.

"Yep," Jack said. "You ever been before?"

"No," said the woman. "This will be our first time."

"Us too," Diane said.

The woman was very pretty. A natural blonde with a natural tan, no hint of orange smears from lotion or creases from a booth. Jack thought Diane was probably glad she didn't burn today. Otherwise, she might have felt a little insecure. Not that she needed to. He'd take his ginger goddess over a bland Barbie doll any day.

"I'm Brett Hinsey," the man said, holding his hand out between the seats to Jack and then Diane. "And this little lady is my wife, Claire."

"Pleased to meet you both," Jack said. He introduced himself and Diane, blushing when he had to correct himself that she was no longer his girlfriend but his fiancée.

Claire smiled and congratulated them. Jack marveled at how

radiant and white her teeth were, as if she polished them at least three times a day. He was mindful of his own coffee and nicotine-stained teeth then, mentally kicking himself for projecting his own insecurities onto Diane. He would have to make it up to her, not that she could read his mind. His own private penance. He wondered which would give out first on this trip: his back or his balls.

The four of them started talking, and the car crept forward.

8:01 PM

BRETT KNEW FROM THE MOMENT he saw them they would be perfect. Claire squeezed his hand, and he knew she felt the same.

They had been trying to shop for souvenirs most of the afternoon. His in-laws would be visiting that weekend. Claire didn't want to give them something they'd wear once or just shove into a closet. The trouble was everything on the boardwalk was generic or trashy. Why her parents felt the need to intrude on their only living child's honeymoon Brett didn't know, but if he wanted that deposit to start his own auto shop in September then he had to keep playing nice.

Neither of them could agree on anything to buy so they decided to put it off until tomorrow. There was a holiday themed store in town they might try. Claire's mother was crazy about sentimental crap like that. Besides, they were thoroughly sick of the boardwalk and starving. That Polish kid or whatever he was hadn't been very filling.

It was Brett's idea to carpool. Claire bitched and moaned, but now he knew she was kicking herself for not coming up with the idea herself. Jack was scrawny like a string bean, and Diane was as hot a piece of ass as he could ask for. More than that, they reminded him of his first kills. It was like this was meant to be. The four of them were getting along nicely. Claire showed Diane pictures from their wedding.

"We almost didn't get the venue," Claire explained. "There was a computer issue or something and it got double booked. Us and another couple who had to postpone their original date because of COVID. But luckily, they had a change of plan, and we got it after all."

Claire had tracked the other couple down through social media and figured out their address. A month before the wedding, very late at night, Claire knocked on their door claiming to have been driving by and seen an unconscious man in their yard. She told them she already called 911 and the dispatcher wanted her to alert them in case the man was a resident. While his fiancée comforted Claire the would-be groom went out to investigate. Brett stopped playing possum and shoved a knife in his throat. By the time he walked through the front door of the house Claire had the woman pinned on her back. "Take your time," she said. And he did.

When they arrived at the restaurant, the hostess said it would be a forty-minute wait for a table, but four seats had just opened at the bar. The two couples continued their conversation over drinks. About Paradise, what they had and hadn't done yet. Brett and Diane both wanted to try parasailing while Jack and Claire were content just to lounge in the sun. Likewise, this was Brett and Diane's first time visiting while Jack and Claire were reliving childhood nostalgia.

"Is it as nice as you remember?" Diane asked.

"Better," Claire said.

Jack agreed. The four of them decided to split an order of Jamaican nachos. Claire sipped a banana daiquiri and asked how Jack and Diane met.

"We've actually known each other since third or fourth grade," Jack said. "But we didn't start dating until we reconnected two years ago."

"It was kind of random," Diane said, explaining how she used to travel for work and ended up sitting next to Jack at his favorite bar.

"Brooke Logan would call that destiny," Claire said dreamily.

"Who?"

"Don't ask," Brett said. "So how long have you two been engaged?"

"Since yesterday," Diane said, and she told them about the

surprise proposal and the horses and the shit, and they were all still laughing when their appetizer arrived and had to catch their breath before ordering their entrées and another round of drinks.

Jack asked about the two of them. Brett let Claire weave a sanitized version of their love story as he finished his White Claw. Both he and Claire had ordered weaker drinks than usual. Jack ended up getting a third Old Fashioned. Diane was done after her second frozen margarita, but Brett didn't think that would be an issue. When Claire told them this was her and Brett's honeymoon, Jack insisted on paying for their drinks.

Dinner was Caribbean and seafood quesadillas for Jack and Diane and the specialty burger for Brett. Claire, who didn't eat bread, only nibbled at her brown stew chicken. They compared notes on other restaurants they'd tried and were all amused to discover they'd eaten at the same place last night.

"Did you get the hunky drunk waiter too?" Diane asked.

"As a matter of fact, we did," Brett said.

When the checks came, Claire said, "Why don't you guys come back to our place for a while? Have a few more drinks and hang out. We could maybe watch a movie or play some boardgames."

Jack and Diane didn't see a reason to say no.

11:29 PM

WAS IT REALLY SO LATE? Diane checked the time on her phone as they took the elevator to the top floor of the complex. She was wide awake and didn't feel the least bit tipsy. The drive from the restaurant had sobered her. As a thank you for paying for their drinks, Brett and Claire insisted on handling costs for the Uber back to their condo.

"You're our guests!" Brett said. "It's only fair."

They really seemed like a nice couple. And they were definitely in love. The way they looked at each other and touched each other casually on the hand or leg or shoulder simply radiated love and devotion. Diane hoped it wasn't just the honeymoon phase. She really did. Relationships could be slowly and painfully torn apart or severed in an instant. It was hard to say which was worse.

Jack whistled when they entered the condo. Diane didn't blame him. It *was* impressive. When they walked into the penthouse, they found themselves in a spacious if messy kitchen area. Four wooden chairs faced the island counter and another four surrounded a matching table. To their right was the laundry room, followed by a narrow hallway that led to a bathroom, then the stairs to the master suite where, according to Claire, there was another bathroom with a jacuzzi, an oceanfront balcony *and* a bayside balcony for watching sunsets. Next to the stairwell was the door to the guest bedroom. In the living room a six-person couch with a chaise lounge was tucked into the corner across from the second oceanfront balcony, directly beneath the other. There was a glass coffee and end table along with a flat screen TV, not to mention an impressive collection of DVDs.

"Sorry about the mess," Brett said, gesturing at the cluttered sink and countertops. He started locking the door behind him. It took him a minute because there were multiple locks. "If we knew we were having company we would have rid up a little."

"How did you find this place?" Diane asked.

"My aunt bought it when they first opened in the eighties," Claire explained. "She's letting us stay here through Labor Day weekend. The family next door is renting theirs for three grand a week, and one of the other units on our floor just sold for six hundred thousand."

Jack whistled again.

"Make yourselves comfortable," Brett said. "We have a full bar. What can I get you to drink? Scotch? Vodka? Beer?"

"Beer would be fine," Diane said. She sat on the couch while Jack began to peruse the DVDs. "Don't be nebby," she whispered.

Claire caught what she said and laughed.

"Nebby? What does that mean?"

"It's just a Pennsylvania-ism for 'nosey.' Like when we call a shopping cart a buggy or a rubber band a gum band. I asked for dippy eggs at breakfast this morning and about died from embarrassment."

"I think that's cute," Claire said, sitting right next to Diane despite the abundance of space on the couch.

Brett approached with four open bottles of Corona in hand, a fresh slice of lime in each of their necks. He distributed the beer and said, "Chug-a-lug." They all clinked their bottles together, pushed down their wedges so the amber liquid fizzed, and drank.

"That's an eclectic collection of movies you have there," Jack said. "Are they yours or your aunt's?"

"A little bit of both," Claire said. "Anything catch your eye?"

"Well, I was just surprised to see *Casablanca* next to *Henry: Portrait of a Serial Killer* is all. It's kind of like going to Barnes & Noble and seeing *Travels with Charley* next to *Cows.*"

"Please don't talk about *Cows*," Diane said, but her interest was piqued. She looked at the movies organized in no discernable order and noticed such feel-good favorites as *The Human Centipede* and *Megan is Missing* mixed in with *Jewel of the Nile* and *Raiders of the Lost Ark*.

"My in-laws are all a little strange," Brett said. "But then again, who isn't?"

The conversation drifted from movies to television. It wasn't as smooth as earlier, and Diane wondered if coming here was a mistake. Despite the cozy atmosphere and their earlier rapport, she was starting to feel uneasy. It came to her that she and Jack were in the company of strangers. No one else knew where they were. She'd been mindful of excessive screen time ever since a productivity seminar Barb from marketing conducted last September, and Jack was practically a Luddite anyway. But other than booking their ride over here she didn't think she'd noticed Claire and Brett take out their phones once.

"How long did you say you two have been together?" Diane asked.

"Gosh, let me think," Claire said. "I guess it was a year in February, right babe?"

"That's right pumpkin," Brett said. He wrapped a beefy arm around her shoulder. "A month before the world stopped turning."

"I'm just glad we were able to get married in-person. I never would have heard the end of it from my mother if we didn't. Same with graduation. Christ that was only, what, two months ago? Time flies."

Diane did some quick math and realized Claire was only twenty-two. No wonder she looked so good. Brett could have been anywhere from the same to early thirties. It was hard to tell with overly muscular men. Still, wouldn't someone Claire's age have been documenting the entire night from start to finish on social media?

"So where do you lovebirds think you'll settle down?" Jack asked.

Brett shrugged. "I really don't know. I moved around the Midwest a lot growing up. I moved even more when I was in the Air Force. I've never really been in one place for too long. Ohio's okay, more or less, depending on where you are. Claire's parents are pushing us to move to Bel Air but the thought of seeing them every week or even just once a month for the rest of my life makes me want to blow my head off with a shotgun."

He and Claire laughed. Jack and Diane glanced at each other, unsure how to respond.

"Where in PA did you say you two grew up?" Claire asked. She had finished her beer but held the bottle close. A little too close. She was rubbing it between her breasts.

Jack cleared his throat and looked away. "A little nowhere town thirty minutes south of Pittsburgh. It's funny. When we were kids both of us couldn't wait to get the hell out of there and never look back. Now it's home again."

Diane supposed this was true. Her apartment in the city was practical, but she wasn't exactly emotionally attached to it. Even though she could afford a house on her own salary alone, she would never ask Jack to give up his childhood home. It was his legacy. A good place to raise a family. The fact she couldn't have biological children was something he insisted didn't bother him. Maybe they'd adopt someday, maybe they wouldn't. It was still too early to tell. Hell, they weren't even married yet.

"Anyone want another beer?" Brett asked.

"No thank you," Diane said. She checked her phone again and saw that it was now already ten minutes until midnight. Her mind searched for an excuse to leave that was both polite and believable.

"Actually, we should probably be heading out," Jack said. He looked at Diane so sheepishly she almost believed what he said next. "I didn't want to spoil the surprise, but I booked us a guided fishing tour for tomorrow morning."

She thought recreational fishing was just about the most boring thing a person could do, although it was nowhere near as unnecessary and barbaric as deer hunting. Jack knew she felt this way just as she knew he was getting as uncomfortable as she was.

"Oh Jack, you shouldn't have," Diane said, making a mental note to show him just how grateful she was when they were back in the safe familiarity of their room.

"Sorry I didn't say anything earlier," Jack said to Brett and Claire. "I guess I just lost track of time."

Brett smiled apologetically. "No worries, man. It happens."

"Let me at least get your phone number," Claire said, searching her pockets. "Maybe we can get together again and … huh."

"Something the matter, sweetheart?" Brett asked.

"My phone. I can't find it."

She stood and turned around, searching between the couch cushions.

"I had it in the car on the ride back. I know I did."

"It probably fell underneath," Jack said. He got down and started to look.

Diane watched Brett and Claire. Something about their expressions, their tones of voice, seemed unnatural. Mechanical. Almost rehearsed.

"Just retrace your steps," Brett said. "You had it when we got in the car. Did you have it in the elevator?"

"I think so."

"Maybe you should call security," Jack said. "See if it's there or in the hall, or if someone else found it and turned it in."

Brett shook his head but was still smiling. "No such luck. Security here is dogshit. They aren't even on sight anymore. They're supposed to be one phone call away, but when we first got here, I tested them. Called to report a prowler. Nobody came by until twelve hours later."

You tested *them*? Diane thought. *Why would you need to do that?*

"What if you just asked them to look at the security feed? I saw the camera in the elevator. It looked old but the red light was blinking."

"They can't check the cameras remotely. The system is way out of date. It hasn't been upgraded since they first opened. They're still on video, which they reuse and tape over at the end of every month since getting new ones is expensive. Plus, they only check old footage if there's a serious reason to do so. Again, I looked into it."

Diane stared at all the locks on the front door, the biggest of which could only be opened by a key, trying desperately to think of a rational explanation for why they would need so many.

"Well, let's go out in the hall and look for ourselves," Diane said, hoping she didn't sound as nervous as she felt. "We'll check there, in the elevator, and the lobby, and if we don't find it you should go ahead and call security anyway. Or do you have a tracker app or something?"

"*No*," Claire said. "No, I *had* my phone when we came home tonight. I *know* I did. It's *here*. It *has* to be."

She enunciated every few words dramatically like an actress on a daytime drama.

"Well, darling," Brett said, standing up and crossing the room toward the stairs. "If you're sure it's here then it's here. I'll check the bedroom and upstairs bathroom. Jack, Diane, could you please help Claire search down here? Thanks."

He was gone before Diane could protest. Claire had gone straight from the front door to the couch almost as soon as they walked in.

There was no way her phone was anywhere else except possibly the kitchen. Diane hadn't been paying attention, but it suddenly occurred to her that if the phone was really missing then Brett should at least try calling it. That way if it was in the condo they would hear it ring or vibrate and if it was back in their Uber then the driver might find it. The mystery would be solved, then she and Jack could leave and forget this whole weird experience and enjoy the rest of their trip in peace.

Jack glanced at her as they poked around the kitchen and knew he was thinking along the same wavelength as her. They didn't find the phone in there, and when an increasingly frazzled Claire was searching in the guest bedroom, their mutual suspicions were confirmed.

"I think she has it," Jack said. "I think she's drunk or high."

"Or both and crazy. What about Brett?"

"He might just be indulging her. He's been upstairs for a while. He's probably used to it and hoping she'll burn herself out."

Diane wasn't sure about that, though Brett did seem to be taking his sweet time. Before they could say anymore Claire came back into the living room with her face in her hands.

"I can't find it anywhere!" she wailed. "It's gone!"

They heard Brett coming down the stairs at last. Diane almost went over to try comforting Claire, but she didn't want to touch her even before she saw that not only was Claire *not* crying, her face wasn't even red.

"It's not upstairs, C," Brett said, scratching at his lower back.

"Then where is it, B?"

"I think you know."

For a moment, Diane thought Jack was right. That Brett was going to apologize to them for all the trouble, find the phone in the back of Claire's waistband then make her take a Xanax and go to bed. Instead, Brett pointed a meaty finger at the two of them and said, "Turn out your pockets."

Diane blinked in disbelief. She looked at Jack and saw his face redden. When he spoke next his voice had a stern edge to it, the tone he probably used with unruly or disrespectful students in the classroom.

"Excuse me?"

"You heard me, faggot."

Diane didn't censor herself. "What the fuck is your problem?"

"My problem is I have a two thieving lying assholes in my home,"

Brett said. "Now give my wife her phone back and nobody gets hurt."

"We don't have her phone! She probably left it in the car, assuming she isn't just hiding it for attention. If this is some kind of prank, it's not funny."

"We're leaving," Jack said. He stood to his full height and looked Brett straight in the eyes. "Unlock the door."

"And what's a pussy like you going to do if I don't?"

"I'm going to call the police and if put your filthy hands on me or Diane I'll break your goddamn arm."

Brett cocked an eyebrow at Claire, who stopped pretending to cry. They grinned at each other like a pair of Jokers from a deck of playing cards.

"What do you think, C? Should we let them go?"

"I don't know, B," Claire purred. "I think he's serious."

"Goddamn right I'm serious," Jack said. "Now I'm not asking you. I'm telling you. Let us go or—"

Before Jack could finish his sentence, Brett had pulled the gun out of his waistband and aimed it between his eyes.

THE THIRD DAY

THURSDAY, JULY 29th, 2021

12:01 AM

THIS ISN'T HAPPENING, **JACK THOUGHT** as Brett herded him and Diane back toward the couch, the gun never straying far from either of their faces. *This is all a misunderstanding. Or a bad joke. There's a hidden camera somewhere and any moment now Ashton Kutcher or Tracy Jordan or whoever the fuck is going to come out, and this will all be over and when they ask us to sign the release waiver, we'll sue them so bad they'll wish they were never born.*

Diane took hold of his hand as they sat down. Jack knew in his pounding heart that yes, this was actually happening. This was real. And he knew as he stared into the abyss of the gun barrel that reason and sanity held no sway in this situation.

Brett settled on the edge of the coffee table, leaning forward so his elbows were on his knees. He made a show of flicking the safety off. Jack didn't know the first thing about firearms, but he recognized the long black cylinder attached at the end of the gun as a silencer.

"So," Brett said after a long pause. "Which one of you has it?"

"Neither of us has your wife's phone," Diane said, keeping her voice steady and calm.

"Now how can I take your word for that, Diane? Empty your

pockets. Slowly."

Jack felt Diane moving beside him and did his best to obey. The air might as well have been molasses. He couldn't have made a sudden movement if he wanted to. They produced their phones, wallets, room keys, a handful of pocket change, his lighter and Winstons, and Diane's spare hair tie. Brett took each object one by one, scrutinized it, then set them aside on the table.

"That everything?" Brett asked, cocking the gun's hammer.

"Yes," Diane said.

Jack was painfully aware that he had not spoken since the gun came out. The guilt that Diane should be handling all the talking made him so sick he almost wanted Brett to shoot him and get it over with. Then the selfishness of that thought and the prospect of leaving Diane to the mercy of these sick freaks turned his cowardice into anger at himself and their captors.

"We don't have the phone," Jack said. "We proved it. Now let us go."

"What's the rush?" Brett asked. "Party's just getting started. Your fishing boat will still be there in the morning."

He winked. Jack's momentary bravado faded almost as quickly as it appeared. Sinking back into the couch, Jack felt the despair drowning him from within again.

"Clearly we made a mistake," Brett said. "You have to understand, my wife is very sensitive, and I can't help but be protective of her. Still, we profusely apologize for any emotional harm this has caused."

"So sorry," Claire said, giggling.

"Let us make it up to you."

Brett stood and handed the gun to Claire, who proceeded to press it against Diane's temple. Without thinking Jack sprung to his feet and screamed, "Point the gun at me!" as Brett pushed him back down without effort.

"Easy. Relax. I'll be right back."

He picked up Jack and Diane's phones, keys, and wallets before sauntering out of the room back upstairs. Claire smiled wider than the Cheshire Cat.

"I'd stay still if I were you, Jack," Claire said. "Next time you might startle me and then I'll blow Diane's pretty red head off. You wouldn't want that, would you?"

Diane remained as still as a statue, glassy brown eyes looking straight ahead. Tears burned in Jack's own.

"Please. Please just let her go. You can do whatever you want to me, just don't hurt her."

"Oh, we will. Do whatever we want to you I mean. The whole letting you go thing depends on how well you behave. And perform, if you know what I mean. So don't blow it."

Brett came trotting back down the stairs. He held a long rectangular box.

"We really feel terrible for inconveniencing you both," Brett said.

"Terrible," Claire said.

"So, to lighten the mood I figured we could play a game."

He tossed the box on the table. Jack had to stare at it for several moments to understand what he was seeing. The idea that this setup was indeed a trashy prank show flickered back into his mind. That or an alcohol and shrimp induced nightmare.

"Monopoly?" Jack asked, dumbfounded.

"Yep. A true classic never goes out of style."

Brett gestured for Claire to give him back the gun. Diane exhaled sharply as it passed between them. She trembled only for a moment then regained her composure. Jack didn't know how she was managing. He felt like a goddamn live wire.

"We play by the book here," Brett said as Claire opened the box and began setting up the board. "No house rules. With one notable exception."

He grinned.

"We pay the bank and other players in clothes instead of cash."

Claire held out a handful of silver playing pieces and said, "I'm always the car and Brett's always the battleship. You can be the shoe or the thimble."

"This is absurd!" Jack said. The red mist descended again. He felt his face and neck blotching as he spoke. "We're not going to sit here and take our clothes off after you threaten and insult—"

"Jack," Diane said.

She looked him in the eyes for the first time since this nightmare started. He saw the fire burning there. Saw her hatred for the people doing this to them, her determination to get out of here alive, and the love she somehow still felt for him despite his inadequacy and big mouth. Her words came out gently even as he watched the flames raging within her.

"Shut the fuck up and take the shoe."

1:46 AM

CLAIRE WAS THE FIRST TO go bankrupt. Diane was pretty sure she did it on purpose. She lay there naked for a while, observing the rest of them. Eventually she got bored and went to fix herself another drink in the kitchen. When she came back, she sat beside Jack and started leaning all over him. Every article of clothing he discarded prompted a new remark. When Jack's shirt came off, Claire squealed.

"Look at the size of those things!"

She grabbed one of Jack's hairy nipples and twisted. He screamed, but the end of Brett's gun jabbing at his chest kept him seated and his hands to himself. They curled into fists at his sides and to Diane's relief they stayed there. Claire was still pulling at his nipples when Jack finally lost the last of his clothes at Brett's railroad, biting her lower lip in anticipation as he pulled down his underwear.

"Urgh, he's uncircumcised! Gross."

She recoiled, moving away from Jack in disgust and drunkenly wobbling over to Brett. The look she gave Diane was a mockery of pity.

By then Diane had most of the utilities and a reasonable number of properties spread across the map. Meanwhile, Brett had built big on the boardwalk and other expensive lots, developing them all to the max. There wasn't much sense in this strategy since they weren't playing for money, but sense didn't matter much to perverted psychopaths. On her next turn, Diane rolled a seven and landed on luxury tax.

Brett held out his free hand. The other stayed on the gun resting in his lap.

"The ring. Take it off."

She sensed Jack about to object and obeyed before he could speak. Brett held it up to the light, squinting at it.

"What is this, a ruby?"

"Garnet," Jack muttered.

"How much?"

Jack held his breath. Diane moved her left foot slightly, so that it was just touching his right. The skin-to-skin contact, however minor, produced the intended effect. He answered before Brett felt the need to raise the gun again.

"One thousand dollars."

"That's a lot of shoes sold."

"I don't work on commission."

"Did you put it on your credit card?"

Jack nodded. Claire whispered something to Brett, and they both laughed.

It doesn't matter, Diane thought. *Money doesn't matter. Don't let this ape fuck with your head, Jack. You're better than him. Smarter. Kinder. Prettier. Hung like a fucking elephant's trunk when you get worked up enough. I love you. Don't fall for their bait. Play along until we can get out. Get help. Get even. Get that gun away from them and—*

"Your turn again, sugar tits," Brett said.

Diane passed go, collected her two hundred—they were still using the paper money for anything collected from the bank because God forbid they be allowed to put their clothes back on—and came to rest on Baltic Avenue, which was in her control.

"Come on, baby," Claire said, rubbing Brett's massive shoulders. "You've got this. You can do it. I believe in you."

She sounded like a cheerleader banging the quarterback before the last big game. As if any of this mattered beyond terrorizing Jack and Diane, prolonging their suffering, maybe even trying to turn them against each other.

Brett rolled two sixes and landed on Oriental Avenue, which had belonged to Jack, but since he was out of the game Brett paid nothing. He was down to just his briefs. Diane still had her bra and underwear. Brett decided to roll again. Two fours this time. That put him on Pennsylvania Railroad.

He contemplated a third roll, decided to go for it, and got snake eyes.

Diane couldn't help smirking. House rules meant he couldn't collect on her until he was out of jail. Since he didn't have a Get Out of Jail Free card, he had three turns to roll doubles again to get out without paying. And since he was down to his underwear, that meant bankruptcy. He was trapped like a rat. She was safe.

Serves you right, you bastard.

"Three doubles," Diane said. "Too bad. Go directly to j—"

In one sweeping gesture Brett knocked the entire board off the table. Paper money and Chance cards went flying. Claire clapped her hands and laughed in delight, but Diane could tell from the vein throbbing in Brett's neanderthal forehead that he was legitimately pissed.

"Boring game anyway," Brett said, grinding his teeth. "Let's play something else."

Jack, who had been cupping his privates in his hands since losing, tentatively reached for his clothes from the discard pile.

Brett aimed his Desert Eagle at the space between Jack and Diane's heads and fired.

The muffled bang made them jump, both trying to shield the other.

"That was a warning," Brett said. "Next time I won't be so nice. You don't move, you don't speak, and you don't get dressed unless one of us tells you to. Understand?"

Jack nodded.

"Come on, B," Claire said. "Let him put his panties back on at least. I'm disgusted just thinking of that wrinkly turtleneck on his dick. I don't want to look at if I don't have to."

"Okay, put the underwear on. But I'm doing this for my wife, not for you."

He watched Jack cover himself, wrinkling his nose in disgust.

"You know one of your balls hangs lower than the other?"

Again, Jack nodded. Brett shook his head and then brightened.

"I know what we should play," he said, giving Claire the gun again before hurrying into the kitchen. Diane didn't dare turn her attention away from Claire to see what he was doing. Brett called out, "We used to play this all the time during basic training. You guys will love it."

He came back to the living room with a dirty and scuffed white cutting board in one hand and a large kitchen knife in the other. He set the board on the table and held onto the knife. Both were glistening wet with flecks of green rind from dicing the lime for their Coronas what felt like a lifetime ago.

"This is much more fun than stuffy old Monopoly. What do you say?"

"You don't need to do this," Diane said, knowing he and Claire just *wanted* to do this. "You've had your fun. Nobody's been hurt. You can let us go and that will be the end of it. We won't tell anyone what happened here. No one would believe us anyway. We're not stupid."

"Neither are we, Diane," Brett said. "Now put your hand on the board."

Jack opened his mouth to speak. Diane could have punched him. Was he *trying* to get killed? She put her left hand down without any further protest.

"You a leftie?" Brett asked.

"No."

"Use your right hand."

Diane obeyed, spreading her fingers apart as wide as she could while Brett spoke.

"Now the way this game works is simple. I take this knife, and I stick the pointy end into the board between your fingers. I go faster and faster until I give up or get you. If you flinch and I cut you, I win. If you stay still and I cut you, you win. Understand?"

"If I win you let us leave," Diane said.

"Maybe we do, maybe we don't. You need to play to find out. Ready?"

Bracing herself, Diane nodded.

"Okay. Here we go."

Thunk.

The knife struck the board between her thumb and index finger.

Thunk.

Now it went between her index and middle.

Thunk thunk.

Brett was looking at her face instead of watching the knife.

"That was just a warm-up," he said. "Time to get serious."

Thunk thunk thunk thunk.

She heard Jack audibly gulp and wished she could squeeze his hand but didn't dare break her concentration.

Thunk thunk thunk thunk thunk thunk thunk thunk.

Claire was giggling again and Diane wanted nothing more than to take the knife from Brett and cut through her pretty throat until she hit bone.

Thunk thunk thunk thunk thunk thunk thunk thunk thunk thunk thunk thunk.

Her eyes couldn't keep up with the blade any longer. She could feel her bladder tightening. The world around her shrunk as the already claustrophobic walls of the condo pressed in on her vision until it was just her and the knife.

Thunk thunk—

Abruptly Brett jammed the knife into the edge of the cutting board beside Diane's hand, a good six inches away from her thumb. He was panting, and when she dared look away from the knife Diane saw that his forehead was dappled with sweat.

"Phew," Brett said. "You are one tough babe. Kudos to you."

I bet you can't even spell 'kudos,' you dumb motherfucker. She had to pee so badly her insides burned. She thought she might even vomit from stress. Flying a 747 in a loop-de-loop would have been preferable to another moment of this savagery.

Brett extracted the knife and held it out with the hilt pointed at Diane.

"Now I know what you're thinking. You'd like a turn. But I'm still not one hundred percent sure you're square with me and Claire. She hasn't found her phone yet, has she? I figure it's only fair she goes next."

He traded his wife the knife for the gun and moved uncomfortably close to Diane. She smelled his breath, stale and sour from old beer and beef from dinner still stuck between his teeth. With surprising care, Brett took hold of Diane's wrist and lifted it from the table. She hadn't realized it was still there.

"I think you've had your fun," he said. "Let Jack have a go at it."

No, Diane wanted to scream. The touch of this thing in a man's skin was bad enough, but she would *not* let him or anyone touch Jack. Gun or no gun from this close she could bite into his neck and rip out his jugular even with a bullet in her torso. Jack was stronger than he looked. He could take the blonde bitch, knife or no knife, call the police, call an ambulance, and even if she didn't make it, at least he would. There was still time for him, still hope, this might be their only chance, all she had to do was open her mouth and go for it.

Jack's hand replaced hers on the cutting board.

She looked at him and could have cried. His face was pale. Instead of the knife or the gun or their tormentors he was looking at her, and the look in his eyes wasn't that of a thirty-year-old man but of the boy six lockers down stealing secret glances at her, too timid to do or say anything back then yet always hoping, always dreaming, always—

Claire stabbed straight through the middle of Jack's pinkie finger.

It came away in a rush of blood and stayed on the board as Jack reared back and howled, his scream piercing Diane's ears and heart. Before she could stop herself, she lunged not for Brett or the gun but at Claire.

"*Bitch!*"

Claire's eyes widened in momentary panic, her jubilation at Jack's pain forgotten. Then Brett grabbed Diane by her hair and jerked her back on the couch. He backhanded her across the face, pressed the gun to her cheek.

"Don't call my wife a bitch," Brett said. "Or I'll shove this gun up your smug cunt, empty the magazine, then reload and do it again."

Jack had fallen to the floor sobbing, holding his bleeding hand under his armpit. He tried to get to his knees but before he could Claire was behind him holding the knife to his throat.

"Let me kill him, B," Claire said.

"Apologize to my wife."

Diane bit the inside of her cheek, fighting back her own tears and mumbled, "I'm sorry."

"Louder!"

"I'm sorry!"

Brett pulled her to her feet so roughly she thought he might dislocate her shoulder. He started dragging her toward the bathroom and said, "I think you could use a time out."

"Diane!" Jack screamed. He tried to get up again, but Claire kicked him in the back. Jack fell forward, hitting his face on the corner of the coffee table.

"Get the zip ties from the laundry room and tie him up," Brett said. "I'll deal with her."

2:17 AM

SHE SAT ON THE TOILET glaring at him.

"Go ahead," Brett said.

Diane had not spoken a word since he separated her from Jack. Fine by him. Let her pout.

"I know you need to go. I can see it in your eyes."

He could see a lot in those eyes actually. It made him nostalgic for his early days, the days before Claire, when he took a different woman or sometimes a girl once or twice a month if he could get away with it. And he did, the incident that got him discharged notwithstanding, and even that was a slap on the wrist compared to what the Air Force could have done to him. Some of them went away inside during. Others fought back start to finish. Most of them cried. And he knew Diane was a fighter. Brett had no preference.

"You're going to get a UTI if you keep holding it in."

Like he'd let her live long enough for that to happen. He knew it. She knew it. He knew that she knew it, and she knew he knew she knew it.

Stalemate.

How to proceed?

Rough lover boy up some more? No, let Claire have fun with him. Whip it out and use it one way or another? Nah, he didn't really need to go and besides, that would come later.

"How about this?" Brett asked. "I'll turn around and close my eyes."

He raised his left hand over his face and half-turned. His right arm remained extended with the gun trained on her.

"No peeking. Promise. I don't look. You don't go for my gun. Everybody wins."

Still no answer.

With a dramatic sigh Brett closed his eyes and hummed tunelessly. The whirring of the overhead vent annoyed him, and not for the first time he wished he could turn it off, but it was connected to the lights. Unlike the upstairs bathroom there was no window. The guest bathroom was cramped and narrow, barely bigger than the laundry room next to it. The sink, toilet, and shower tub were all standard, taking up about half the space. He and Claire didn't use this one much, so everything was still white and pristine. Other than cleanliness the only thing it had over the master bathroom was the closet. Its door was thin and opened with ease, unlike its counterpart, which was heavy and stuck easily. Since the door to the upstairs bathroom opened inward, if the closet door was already opened it would jam and not budge an inch. If Brett was looking for something in that closet like a towel or sunscreen and Claire tried to get in, she'd be kept waiting until he could force the closet shut.

Eventually, he heard a thin trickle that soon became a steady stream. Brett kept his word and didn't move a muscle, not even cracking a smile. *Don't want her thinking I'm some kind of pervert*, he thought. When it stopped, he waited, and there was the expected tearing of toilet paper and then the toilet flushing. After another beat, he asked, "You decent?"

Diane remained silent.

Brett lowered his hand and faced her again. Her underwear was back in place. That was fine. He'd have all the time in the world to look at what was beneath it later. But what to do until then? He wished he could hear what was going on in the living room, but the goddamn vent was too loud. He wondered what Diane had been thinking about while he wasn't looking. How to kill him probably. Her options were limited. The mirror would take too long to break and there was no guarantee of getting a shard big enough to cut him effectively. The plunger and scrub brush were a joke. Maybe the shower rod could be used as a blunt instrument, or she could choke him out with the detachable shower head.

That gave him an idea.

"Did you wipe enough?" Brett asked. "I don't mean to be rude. You can never be too careful about keeping clean."

Diane said nothing.

"You know, I used to hate baths as a kid. Did you? I bet you did. My mother loved them though. Stop me if you've heard this one before, but she saw *Psycho* on TV as a little girl and was scared to death of showers. May God strike me dead if I'm lying."

He was of course, and Diane probably knew that, but she didn't budge from her position as he pulled open the shower curtain and put the rubber stopper in the drain. God didn't do anything either.

"I'm sorry I didn't think of this sooner," Brett said, which was the truth. "Otherwise, I'd have prepped the jacuzzi upstairs. But I think this will do just fine."

Diane still didn't say anything.

Brett held the Desert Eagle at his hip and said, "Get in."

Slowly, like a zombie rising from the grave, Diane got up from the toilet and sat down in the tub. She wasn't looking at the gun anymore. She wouldn't look at him either, not even when he took down the shower head and held it over her. Her lips didn't so much as tremble.

You bitch, Brett thought. He felt The Urge rising but kept it in check. *You miserable uptight bitch. Think you're better than me? I'll show you. Ice cold, huh? This will thaw you out. Melt you down.* He imagined her shrieking *I'm melting, melting, ooh what a world!* and himself singing, *Ding-dong, the bitch is dead! Which old bitch? The wicked bitch*, as he explained the rules of this new game to her.

"I'm going to test your endurance now. You don't want to talk to me? Fine. I'm going to give you a nice hot bath and you're going to lie there and take it. If you make so much as a peep, I'll shoot you in the stomach and fuck the hole until you bleed to death. And believe me, that will take a long time."

Diane closed her eyes.

He turned the hot water on full blast.

2:24 AM

"YOU DON'T HAVE TO DO this."

Claire snorted. She'd put her clothes back on and sat perched on the arm of the couch fingering the tip of the knife, studying Jack like an artist contemplating a block of clay.

"Don't have to do what?"

"We can help you," Jack said. "If he's hurting you, making you do this, it'll be easier. The police will understand. We'll even testify on your behalf."

What stage of grief was bargaining again? Claire could never remember. Regardless, it was a close second to her least favorite of all, acceptance. Denial, anger, and depression were all much more interesting.

"You know," Claire said, examining a drop of blood that had welled from her fingertip. "I think it's really sexist of you to assume I'm an unwilling accomplice or brainwashed victim."

She sucked on her finger thoughtfully.

"I didn't mean to offend you. That was completely out of line. I apologize."

He squirmed. She'd used the zip-ties to bind his hands behind his back and around the leg of the coffee table. His ankles were likewise bound. When he smacked his face against the table earlier, Jack split his right eyebrow and bottom lip wide open. The blood had flowed in abundance. Head wounds always did.

"There have been a lot of great female psychopaths, you know," Claire lectured. "Elizabeth Bathory. Aileen Wuornos. Sheila Carter."

The last was her favorite fictional character, the greatest soap opera villain of all time, but if Jack knew who she was he didn't feel the need to comment.

Claire continued, "My parents are assholes but not in any way that contributed to the predicament you currently find yourself in. Daddy didn't fuck me. Mommy didn't hit me. As for Brett, did it ever cross your mind that we could be equals in this operation? A marriage *is* a partnership. It's the 2020s, not the 1920s. You'd better remember that if you ever want to tie the knot with Little Red Riding Whore. Assuming she still wants your weird dick after Brett's done with her. How many times do you think he's made her come so far?"

"Cunt," Jack hissed. "You're an evil fucking cunt."

There's anger, Claire thought. She climbed off the couch and kneeled before Jack, dangling the knife in front of him like a carrot on a stick.

"What do you want to do to me, Jacky? You want to jam this up inside me and twist it?"

"You wish."

"I'll tell you a secret," Claire whispered. "Brett doesn't even know about this. I've used his gun to masturbate before. Think if he makes Diane suck on it, she'll taste me and like it?"

Jack spat in her face.

"Cunt."

"I'm going to carve that word into your forehead if you keep using it."

She wiped her cheek and brushed the hair out of Jack's face. He tried to pull away but there was nowhere to go. Claire had one knee on his groin to keep him breathless and steady, applying more pressure as she spoke.

"David Kimble got the word 'Killer' cut into his forehead during botched plastic surgery in 1991, not long before he went down a garbage chute and got crushed to death. Supposedly. They only found one arm. He could always come back to Genoa City someday. He was before my time, but my grandma had it all recorded on VHS. I probably still have the tape somewhere."

Claire started tracing words with her finger on his face.

"I might do 'Fag.' Three letters. Nice and easy. I bet they called you that a lot in high school. To your face *and* behind your back. I'm sure Diane did, not that she'd admit it now. I wonder what happened to make her give up and settle for a loser like you anyway. Maybe I'll ask her if she's not already dead. They've been in the bathroom a long time."

Jack's teeth snapped at her probing finger. She pulled it away just in time.

"What else did they call you? They had to have called you something. People like you were always given a nickname. Jack-Off? No, that's too easy. Jack the Jerk? Too tame. You don't have any acne scars or excess skin, so nothing pimple related and no fat jokes. Let's see. Something about your foreskin or maybe those big pepperoni nipples?"

At the word "nipples" Jack's face twitched. Claire knew she had him.

"That's it, isn't it? Tell me what they called you."

He started to cry.

"No."

"Tell me or I'll slice your dick down the middle."

Jack mumbled.

"I can't hear you."

"Nips!" Jack said, snot dripping down his nose. "They called me Nips."

"Did Diane ever call you Nips?"

Glumly, Jack nodded. Claire removed her knee from his crotch and leaned back, sitting cross legged in front of him. She put a fist under her chin and pretended to be deep in thought.

"Gosh, that's too bad, Jacky Boy. Kids can be so cruel. I wish there was something I could do to help you."

She gasped dramatically, looking back and forth between his chest and her knife.

"I know! Plastic surgery. Why didn't I think of it sooner?"

"No," Jack said, eyes wide. He resumed his earlier attempts to break free of his binds with much more gusto. "No, stay back. Stay the fuck away from me!"

Claire sprung to her feet and skipped into the kitchen. She grabbed a roll of paper towels and a bottle of Absolut from the freezer, stopping to check her phone for any messages. She'd tucked it into a drawer when Jack and Diane weren't paying attention when they first arrived at the condo. There weren't any, so she returned it to its hiding place and went back to the living room where Jack was still screaming himself hoarse.

"Help! Someone help us!"

"That's not going to do any good," Claire said, splashing vodka onto the knife blade. "Security here is shit but the soundproofing isn't. Too bad for you. Now hold still."

She leaned down and slashed Jack's right nipple and was surprised by the spurt of blood that sprayed her face. His scream rose in pitch, and he thrashed so badly her second swing cut him across the middle of the chest. She felt the blade scrape against his ribcage.

"*Hold still, goddammit.*"

Claire straddled him, grateful she remembered to reseal the cap on the vodka in case he managed to knock it over. Those two-liter bottles weren't cheap. Her third slash made a nice X across his right nipple. She made a cute little cross on his left with her fourth and fifth. Her sixth took it clean off. Jack mewled like a kitten. The sound of his screeching actually started to hurt her ears. Claire felt a migraine coming on.

"Alright, you big baby. God. I was only trying to help."

She got off him again and picked up the vodka. It was almost empty, and Claire was irritated she'd bothered to waste any sanitizing the knife. Not like a dead man could get an infection. On the bright side, at least it probably made his cuts burn more. She chugged what was left and dropped it, letting the empty bottle roll away. Jack was bent over and blubbering almost as bad as her little brother had when she killed him. That at least managed to brighten her mood. Not wanting Jack to bleed to death yet, Claire pressed his wounds with the roll of paper towel, hushing him and telling him everything would be okay, just like she'd done with her brother.

Claire's eyes wandered to the end table. They'd left Jack and Diane's clothes piled up beside it, except for the engagement ring, which was now on Claire's right hand. It was nothing compared to the giant diamond on her wedding finger, but that wasn't the point. The phones and wallets were in Brett's bedroom nightstand, in the same drawer that normally stored the Desert Eagle. All of it would have to be destroyed of course, just like the Ohio license Claire still had in her purse. Not to mention what was left of the waiter.

She left Jack still crying and bleeding to steal one of his cigarettes, had just lit it and was still holding the lighter, looking at the little flame dance when she had another idea.

Claire knew *exactly* how to stop his bleeding.

2:41 AM

BY NOW THE SCALDING WATER had surpassed Jack's screams in causing her agony, but still Diane would not make a sound. She would die before she gave Brett the satisfaction. And she would die very soon. Of that she was certain.

Her hands gripped the sides of the tub. She closed her eyes and thought of the beach and the sand and the cold ocean as steam filled her lungs. When she woke up that morning, she'd worked out like she always did, watched a beautiful sunrise with her fiancé and made love, ridden a bicycle, gone sight-seeing, tanned and swam in the ocean, napped and had more sex and watched a bad movie. How could such a perfect day lead to this?

"Hot enough for you?" Brett asked, blasting her in the face.

He'd been alternating spraying her hot and cold, perhaps realizing boiling her alive would be impractical if not downright impossible using a regular bath and showerhead. And even if he could do it, third degree burns would probably kill his erection before they killed her. Diane felt wrapped in a cocoon of sweat. Her soggy skin was red and raw. If she stayed in any longer, she thought it might start peeling. The water in the tub overflowed. It splashed over the edges and made

Brett step back, nearly slipping more than once.

If he could just fall, she would be up and on him before he knew it. She'd go for his eyes and then for his gun and while he was writhing on the floor, Diane would go out into the living room, shoot Claire, then come back in and finish him off. She thought about splashing and blinding him that way, but knew he'd pull the trigger before she could.

Brett turned off the showerhead. He let it fall into the bath instead of hanging it back in place. He stood over Diane, tapping his thigh with the gun.

"You are one tough bitch," Brett said. "I thought for sure you'd break. Maybe I should have brought your boyfriend in here. He'd have squealed for sure. Just listen to him out there."

Jack's cries continued to carry over the throbbing in her ears and the rattle from the ceiling vent. Brett let out a dreamy sigh.

"Claire really is something."

He kneeled, leaning over the tub.

"I'll let you come out of the bath on one condition."

Diane refused to even blink.

"You've done well so far, but I have one more test. I think you can manage it. I'm going to push your head under the water now, and I want you to hold your breath until I let you go. If I see any bubbles, you're not coming back up. On the count of three now."

I am going to kill you.

"One."

The thought was calm and clear. Despite the pain and the knowledge Brett could easily just shoot her and get it over with, Diane knew he wouldn't. Whether it was ego or pride or lust, she didn't care. Motive didn't matter. Nothing else he did tonight mattered.

"Two."

She was going to kill him and his wife the first chance she got, slowly and painfully if she could, and if not, it didn't matter because she would still be alive and they would be dead and if there was a God, they'd be rotting in hell getting raped and skinned for eternity.

"Three."

Diane took the deepest breath of her life, closed her mouth and eyes just before Brett shoved her head underwater. He held it there.

Minutes passed.

She thought of Jack.

3:06 AM

JACK MUST HAVE BEEN DREAMING.

He blacked out when the burning started and had been drifting in and out of consciousness since. The stink of cooked pork and burnt hair choked him awake every few minutes. The realization that it came from his own chest hit him with renewed shock every time. His head swam with vertigo. At some point, his stomach spasmed and he puked until there was nothing left inside him, but his muscles still ached as if squeezed by an invisible hand trying to wring him dry. He kept trying to tell himself that at some point he would open his eyes and be in the nice soft bed back at the hotel with the worst hangover of his life. His body would be intact. Diane would be there to comfort him. He would forget this nightmare ever happened.

"Wakey, wakey, sleeping beauty."

Jack moaned, turning away. Claire grabbed him by his face and shook him until he opened his eyes.

"Look who came to visit."

Claire stepped away and Jack suddenly felt wide awake. Diane stood before him soaking wet and trembling, her perfect skin as pink as if she'd been badly sunburned. Brett was holding her up by the arm and when he saw Jack was awake, he smiled and let her drop to the floor.

Diane collapsed on her side, blinking through red eyes and coughing as she took deep, shuddering breaths.

"I have to admit," Brett said. "I'm impressed. Your Little Mermaid here managed five whole minutes underwater without a single breath."

"Bastard," Jack whispered. He ignored the pain and pressure in his hands from the zip ties digging into his wrists. He leaned forward, desperate to reach Diane. To touch her, feel her, comfort her and take comfort in return. If they were going to die the least these monsters could do was let them die together.

He watched Diane gradually catch her breath, saw her pupils fix on him and widen as they comprehended the smoldering black and red ruin that had been his chest. She reached out to him automatically, stopping just short of touching his wounds. Diane rose to her knees and caressed his cheek instead.

"How sweet," Claire said. "I just love happy endings, don't you?"

Diane stiffened. Jack reluctantly turned his gaze to Brett and Claire, who were standing shoulder to shoulder looking down on them with the detached indifference of children burning ants under magnifying glasses. Brett had tucked his gun down the front of his shorts. Claire was still playing with her knife, Jack's blood drying on her face.

"You two just hang tight," Brett said. "Me and the missus need to have a private conversation. Don't try anything stupid while we're gone."

They disappeared upstairs, Brett in the lead and Claire giggling as she followed him. They saw her smack his ass before they were completely out of sight.

Jack stopped straining. His shoulders slumped forward.

"We're going to die," he said. "We're going to die and it's all my fault."

"No, we're not and no it isn't," Diane growled. Her eyes frantically searched the room.

"It's hopeless. You saw how many locks are on the front door. The keys are in his pockets. He'll blow our heads off before we get close."

Diane was looking at the empty vodka bottle Claire had carelessly let roll away.

"I could break that open and hold it to her throat," Diane said.

"He'd shoot you before you had the chance."

"Him then. I'll jam it in his face when he comes back down."

"Then she'll stab you in the back. You can't take them both."

"The hell I can't."

Footsteps. Too late to do anything now.

Brett and Claire returned looking as chipper as ever. They were holding hands, swinging their arms back and forth between them. Brett had changed into a new set of clothes.

"Okay," Brett said. "You can go now."

For one long moment Jack and Diane didn't move.

"Come on. We don't have all night long. Let's get a move on."

"Honey," Claire said. "I think Jack might need a little help."

"Of course! Where are my manners? Sorry. I'm pretty tired."

He took Claire's knife and began to approach. Diane practically threw herself on top of Jack, who bit back a scream when she inadvertently touched his burns.

"No," Diane said. "I don't trust you."

"That's understandable," Brett said. "Given the circumstances."

He dropped the knife at her feet and backed away, palms raised outward.

Diane watched him carefully for a moment and set about cutting Jack loose. The blood rushing back into his hands and feet caused him the best pain he'd felt in hours. He welcomed it, appreciated it, wiggling his toes and fingers for the sheer thrill of being able to do so. Together, he and Diane helped one another to their feet. Jack was still dizzy. He caught a glimpse of his left nipple in a puddle of blood on the floor and thought he might be sick again. Diane gripped his hand almost as tightly as she did the knife.

"You're probably wondering why we've decided to be so magnanimous," Brett said.

Actually, Jack was wondering if Brett read a thesaurus looking for four syllable words to sound smarter or if Claire wrote out his lines before they did their abduct and torture routine.

"Originally, we had a whole different third act planned out for this," Brett continued, speaking directly to Diane as though Jack wasn't there. "I was going to take Nips for a little car ride. I'd make him get dressed again obviously. Cross over the state line into Virginia, not saying a word or even playing anything on the radio. Then I'd turn right around and drive back into town. Real mind fuck shit."

"B loves psychological warfare," Claire said.

"I was going to tell him to open my glovebox, where I keep a second gun. Tell him if he didn't shoot the next person we saw on the street, I'd kill you when we got back, make him watch, big moral dilemma. When obviously he'd just try to shoot me, which is why that gun isn't loaded. Great on paper but with several glaring logistical issues, most of all being that dragging this out any longer would be boring."

Claire sighed in disappointment.

"I'm the problem. All I could think of for us to do while the boys were out having their fun was make you watch *The Princess Bride* with me. But I'm so sleepy I don't think I could manage it."

She put her head on her husband's shoulder.

"I'm sorry for letting you down, B."

"You couldn't if you tried, C," Brett said, patting her on the back. "Every game ends eventually. Go ahead and get dressed now. We'll keep your phones and your wallets. If you tell the cops anything about us, we know where you live. By the time they get here, any evidence will have been destroyed. You'll look crazy, and even if they believed you, you know we have the money to beat any charges. So, let's just call this whole thing a draw and say goodnight."

They're just going to shoot us in the back as soon as we start putting our clothes back on or when we're walking toward the front door, Jack realized. This was just one last cheap effort to provoke a reaction out of them. Make them cling to a final shred of hope. It was beyond idiotic. A quick glance at Diane told him she'd figured the same.

He evaluated their limited options.

Rushing Brett and Claire, even with the knife, would just bring the bullets even faster. Playing along with the charade could have merit if the two were willing to wait for them to head for the exit. They probably wouldn't expect them to run into the guest room or up the stairs, but that momentary surprise wouldn't earn Jack and Diane anything more from Brett and Claire than incredulous laughter. Both of those paths led to dead ends.

Jack remembered the empty vodka bottle. It really wasn't that far away on the floor. If he pretended to stumble and fall, he might be able to grab it and toss it at one of their heads. Diane could use the opportunity to stab one of them, and if Jack could get back up fast enough, he could attack the other. But who to distract and how to communicate this plan to Diane?

"Well," Brett said. "What do you say? No hard feelings?"

Diane squeezed Jack's hand. He looked at her, and as she spoke, he followed her eyes from the floor to Brett and knew her mind had concocted the exact same plan as his only with more certainty.

"Thank you," Diane said. "Thank you and your wife for your kindness."

Brett smiled in triumph, clearly thinking he'd fooled them.

You. You. Your wife.

Translation to Jack: *Throw the bottle at him. I'll stab him. You tackle her.*

At least, that's what he hoped she meant.

Slowly, with equal reluctance, Jack and Diane let go of each other and began gathering their clothes. They didn't look away from Brett and Claire, who likewise kept their eyes on them. Their saccharine expressions were infuriating, but if Brett's hands stayed away from his gun their plan had the faintest chance of succeeding. Jack's heart pounded, the force of it sending more waves of pain through his brutalized chest, but for the first time since this nightmare started his mind remained focused.

Diane had pulled on her shorts and blouse, working on the buttons with one hand as she kept the knife in Brett and Claire's sight line.

Jack didn't need much to fake his fall. He stepped into his pants, hiked them up to his hips, and pretended to slip in his own blood and vomit that were both still wet and warm on the floor. It got him within grabbing distance of the bottle neck and didn't appear to raise Brett and Claire's suspicions in the least. They were underestimating him to their peril.

"Come on, slowpokes," Brett said, eyes still on Diane. "Let's get a move on."

Jack was about to grab the bottle when someone knocked on the front door.

3:15 AM

NONE OF THEM MOVED. AFTER a brief pause the knocking resumed, more insistent.

"Who the fuck is that?" Claire quietly snarled through clenched teeth, her widened eyes betraying her terror in a way Diane found immensely satisfying.

"I don't know," Brett whispered.

The knocking continued more aggressively, a muffled voice coming through. Diane strained to hear. Whoever it was, it sounded like they were saying, "I know you're in there."

"Jesus," Claire said. "Is that—?"

Brett nodded, looking as annoyed as his wife was frightened. He waved the gun in Jack and Diane's general direction without really looking at them.

"Not one word from either of you or I kill that asshole and his entire fucking family. Give me back the knife. Drop it and kick it over. Now."

Diane's stomach lurched. She did as he instructed, knowing that if not for the person at the door, Jack would have hurled the bottle at Brett's ugly face. Her dream of plunging the knife that had mutilated her beloved under the brute's ribcage into his heart was shattered. The air between her and Jack that had seemed to crackle with psychic electricity moments ago went static. They could only wait and see if this interruption saved or damned them.

3:16 AM

BRETT TUCKED THE KNIFE INTO his pocket, pulled out the gun, turned off the safety, and held it behind his back as he set about unlocking everything but the chain at the top of the door. He forced a smile and squeezed the key to the padlock in his other hand hard enough to draw blood as he greeted his neighbor.

"Morning, Dan," Brett said. "What seems to be the trouble?"

The portly middle-aged man glowered at Brett through bloodshot eyes ringed by heavy purple lids. Brett could see a vein twitching under his right eye. Dan was unshaven, wearing only a wife beater and striped boxers. Clearly, he'd just been roused out of bed.

"Do you know what time it is, mate?" Dan asked.

"Gosh," Brett said. "I don't really know. Why do you ask?"

"It's quarter past three in the bloody morning. Janine's been up to feed Adam and says she's heard screaming through the walls. Violet's got insomnia, and says she heard it too, and she ain't never agreed with her stepmum about nothing. Janine's been crying worse than Adam has and telling me I should call the police."

Perfectly soundproof, my fucking ass, Brett thought. He was going to strangle Claire's aunt the next time he saw her.

"Well, I can assure you there's no need to do that. I don't hear anything now, do you?"

If those cocksuckers tried yelling for help Brett would put one bullet in Dan's face, another in Jack's throat, a third in Diane's stomach with the intent to follow through on his earlier threat, then a fourth in that sniveling cow Janine, a fifth in Violet and a sixth in Adam. He'd save the last two for himself and Claire. He had no desire to go out like Bonnie and Clyde, and the thought of his Claire growing old alone in prison filled him with more hatred for everyone who wasn't her than he had ever felt before.

There was movement behind him and the sound of running water in the kitchen.

"Right," Dan said. "See, I told her she was being unreasonable, but Janine has it in her head it was a woman she heard screaming and thinks you've been beating up on Claire."

"That's ridiculous. I'd rather die than hurt Claire."

"That's what I told her, Bart. But you know how birds are. She said I couldn't come back in until I've seen and spoken with you both and I'm sure Claire is okay."

"I'm right here," Claire said, shouldering Brett out of view.

He had a moment of panic, remembering the blood on her face, then saw that she'd quickly managed to scrub it off at the kitchen sink. Claire smiled and worked her magic on the Cockney bastard.

"I think I know what Janine heard. We were watching *American Psycho*, and you know Brett can't hear too well because of the injury he got overseas when he was serving in the Air Force, so we had the volume turned all the way up. The walls are supposed to be soundproof, so we didn't think anyone would mind. We're so sorry to have scared her like that."

Dan bought it hook, line, and sinker. He apologized, promised to put Janine's mind at ease, and told them to get some chocolate frosty milkshakes before bed, whatever the fuck that meant. Brett closed and relocked the door, putting the key back into his pocket.

"Baby, I love you more than words," he said, pushing Claire against the wall and greedily kissing her mouth and neck, mumbling "I love you" over and over again into her hair and skin.

Claire moaned, stroking his gun with one hand and his cock with the other. "Let's kill them next. Let's rent a boat and take them out as far as we can for some fun."

The idea and Claire's frantic touch had Brett ready to blow his load, when he remembered they still had tonight's game to finish. He'd shoot Jack and Diane in the head and be done with it. They'd get rid of their bodies eventually. The waiter's too. Tonight, Brett wanted to fuck his wife until the sun came up. With effort, Brett turned away from Claire to get it over with already.

The living room was empty.

Jack and Diane were gone.

3:21 AM

"FUCK!"

They heard Brett and Claire scrambling downstairs. Doors were slammed open. It even sounded like the couch was overturned.

"Hurry," Diane said.

She and Jack were searching the master bedroom for their phones. They'd heard enough of Brett and Claire's conversation with the British man to know he had at least two children, and there was no doubt in either of their minds that if they called out to him for help it would only get more innocent people killed. Creeping up the stairs unheard as Claire gave her spiel about watching a movie too loud had been like playing the evilest version of red-light green imaginable.

Diane pulled out the last drawer of the dresser while Jack rifled through the closet.

"Not here," Jack said.

She looked up, scanning the room.

"The nightstands."

They were on either side of the bed, perfectly ordinary looking like the rest of the room. A matching set. She and Jack were about to look in both at the same time when they heard footsteps rapidly ascending the stairs.

Jack moved away from his nightstand, wielding the vodka bottle by its neck. Diane pulled hers open and found nothing of use. She was about to climb over the bed to search inside the other when the first bullet whizzed up the stairwell. It struck the closed bathroom door, sending splinters bursting into the air.

"Motherfucker," Brett called out. "I see your fucking shadow on the wall."

The element of surprise partly lost, Jack tossed the bottle as hard as he could without exposing anymore of his body than he had to.

Whether it shattered against the wall or flesh Diane didn't know, but the glass broke. Brett swore and must have stumbled into Claire. One of them or both fell down several steps, Claire yelping in surprise or pain or both. Diane managed to cross over to Jack and pull him away from the doorway, afraid of more impending gunfire.

"What do we do now?" Jack asked.

Diane's head whipped around. Other than hiding under the bed or in the closet, there were the two opposing balconies and the master bathroom. The oceanfront balcony looked identical to its lower twin, from the deck furniture to the sliding glass door. A sign beside the door to the innocuous bayside balcony read "NO ROOFTOP ACCESS." Depending on how private the balconies were, and the distance between them and a neighboring unit's, Diane thought she could climb or jump over to the next-door balcony. Her adrenaline was pumping at full capacity. She could do it. But with his injuries, Jack would never manage it. He'd be standing in plain view. And there was no guarantee she'd end up on one connected to an occupied condo. She didn't know which side the British man had come from.

"The bathroom," Diane said. "We'll barricade ourselves in and scream for help."

The plan wasn't just bad. It was suicidal. But if she was going to die, Diane wanted to die in Jack's arms. They'd slit their wrists or swallow pills. The only other alternative for killing themselves was jumping from one of the balconies together to the ground below.

Diane opened the bathroom door, pushed Jack inside and hurried after him. She shut the door, locked it and stepped back, intending to examine its thickness. The bullet hadn't broken through the other side, so clearly it was fairly solid.

That was when she noticed the closet.

She'd had one just like it in the townhouse with Andrea. They'd both complained about it sticking yet done nothing to fix it. Hoping the same was true of Brett and Claire, Diane heaved it open. She felt its weight, heard the creaking rust of its base and knew it would buy them more time. She didn't know if she should laugh or cry.

Jack groaned behind her, and Diane realized three things in quick succession.

The first was that the light had been left on, which was what allowed her to notice the closet in the first place. The second was that the fan was also on. It wasn't as loud as the one downstairs, which was probably why she hadn't heard it from the bedroom.

The third was the sweet rancid stench of decay.

Diane turned.

The bathroom was an orgy of gore, and the centerpiece was the jacuzzi. It was filled with blood and body parts. A bloated torso floated amongst entrails, its severed and equally waterlogged limbs bobbing amongst other offal she could not identify on sight. On the edge of the tub beside a broken hacksaw was a man's head, kept out of the water. The flesh was slack and gray. It looked familiar. Before Diane could recognize it, she was distracted for the second time that night by fists pummeling a door.

3:24 AM

BRETT SLAMMED HIS SHOULDER INTO the door a third time. The dent was negligible.

"Goddammit!"

"Shh! You want that fuck from next door to come back?"

"Fuck him!" Brett said. "Fuck him and his fucking wife and fuck these fucking fuckers in my fucking bathroom!"

His face was red with blood. The bottle had caught him square in the forehead. He probably had a concussion. Tears gleamed in the corners of his eyes. Her big strong husband was injured and crying, and it was all her fault. Claire's heart broke with guilt. She felt stupid. She would make Jack and Diane pay for doing this to her and B. She wrapped her arms around him.

"Settle down, baby. We'll get them."

Brett sniffled. "I don't want to get caught. I don't want to lose you."

"You're not going to lose me," Claire said firmly. She pushed down her own doubts and tried to think logically. "They didn't find their phones. The police aren't coming. The bathroom wall faces the bay balcony, so if they bang on the walls no one will hear it. They're trapped. We'll starve them out if we need to."

"We can't wait that long! Your parents are coming on Saturday, remember?"

Claire had completely forgotten.

She grabbed the gun out of Brett's hand and fired three shots at the door. Brett snatched it back before she could fire a fourth.

"It's no use, C," Brett said. "Even if one of those got through that piece of shit closet door is in the way, slowing it down. I heard them open it. No hope of a ricochet hitting them, and they're probably not dumb enough to be standing in front of it anyway. Probably."

"What are we going to do now?" Claire wailed.

Brett was thinking, his face screwed up in concentration. Minutes passed, Claire picturing her parents getting in their Mercedes and making the drive from Bel Air with their tiny Republican minds devoid of any thoughts except eating expensive dinners and the least tactful way to ask when they were going to get grandchildren, only to find out when they arrived that their perfect little girl was a thrill killer. She knew she was rich, white, and pretty enough to get away with it. Her parents would pay for the best defense lawyers in the country, assuming they didn't figure out about her brother, but that would mean pinning everything on Brett. And Claire wouldn't allow that. She'd kill her parents first. She'd kill everyone and everything until it was just the two of them and only them until the end of time.

"I've got it," Brett said finally. "I'll pick the lock. Then I ought to be able to open it enough to slip in a screwdriver through the gap and pop the hinge pins out, pull it right off the frame. We can smash through the closet afterwards."

"Baby, you're a genius!" Claire said, throwing her arms around his neck and covering his bloody face in kisses.

He gently pulled free of her embrace and looked around the room. "Now where the hell is my toolbox?"

3:56 AM

JACK AND DIANE SAT HUDDLED TOGETHER on a pile of towels in the corner of the room, watching as the his and hers sinks overflowed from the marble countertops.

Their hope was that Brett and Claire might slip and crack their heads open should they rush in. *When* they rushed in, Jack mentally corrected himself. It was going to happen eventually. They tried to find some electrical appliance in the closet like a hair dryer to shock them with for good measure. As if he and Diane could *Home Alone* themselves out of this mess.

But of course, any necessities had been moved to the guest bathroom downstairs while Brett and Claire left their previous victim to marinate. If it weren't for the small open window in the upper right corner of the room, above the jacuzzi, the putrid odor from its internal gases probably would have knocked Jack and Diane out by now. He'd recognized the waiter immediately. If Diane did, she didn't mention it.

"What would you have named our kids?" Diane asked. "If I could have them."

This was not the subject Jack would have liked to spend their final moments discussing. He didn't even have to make peace with the matter when Diane told him about her infertility. It wasn't a sacrifice in the grand scheme of things for him like she thought it was, no matter how often he'd reassured her. She was enough for him. More than enough.

"Something from a novel probably," Jack said eventually. "One we both liked."

"John Steinbeck then."

"Okay. Jim after the protagonist of *In Dubious Battle* for a boy. Molly after the Nazi killer in *The Moon is Down* for a girl."

"I like that."

They sat in silence for several minutes.

"I never got around to Tolstoy," Diane said.

"Me neither. I did manage *Crime and Punishment*, but it took me a whole month to get through, so I kept putting off *The Brothers Karamazov*."

"Do you think there are books in heaven?"

"I don't think there is a heaven. I want there to be, but I don't think there is."

"I appreciate your honesty. I always have."

Jack kissed her earlobe. He knew it tickled but figured a tickle was the nicest distraction from impending death he could manage. He was starting to feel clammy. His wounds were probably getting infected, not that he'd live to be sick.

"I thought I loved you back then," Jack said. "I looked forward to seeing you in the hallway every morning and between classes, sitting near you in assemblies. But I didn't really know what love was until we'd been seeing each other for a month. We were just sitting down for dinner and talking. I don't even remember what about. Then it hit me that you were a person with your own aches and scars and wants and dreams. I knew it intellectually of course, but that was when I really *felt* it, and since then I've wanted nothing more than to soothe your pain and make you happy. I just want you to be happy."

This is it, Jack thought. *My big dramatic dying speech*. He would be a rambling cliché until the very end.

Diane stood abruptly and crossed the room, careful not to slip. She started looking through the cupboard under the sink and in the closet again.

"There has to be something, anything in this room we can use," she said, throwing aside cleaning products and more towels. "We are *not* dying in here."

Contradicting her was pointless. They were hopeless. There was nothing more for them to do and nothing waiting for them after. Jack couldn't stand the sight of her continued denial. He looked at the dismembered man in the jacuzzi, at the blood splattered wall, at the open window above the body.

The open window.

He struggled to his feet. Diane stopped what she was doing and moved to help him.

"What floor are we on again?" Jack asked.

"The eleventh."

"This is the top floor, yeah?"

Diane nodded.

Jack was trying to remember what the building looked like from the outside. To remember the layout of the entire condo based on what little he had seen in the cover of night. What did the sign to the bay balcony say? NO ROOF ACCESS. They were just below the roof. If they could get up there—

They'd be trapped on the roof. There was probably a stairwell that maintenance workers used to get up there to repair air conditioning units and whatever else was on the roof, but it was almost certainly kept locked from the outside. He was about to say never mind when he heard it.

The lock turned.

The bathroom door creaked open.

They heard the sound of metal on metal. A screwdriver? Then two swift blows from a hammer. Something small hit the floor. The process repeated, and the door rattled in its frame.

"Fee-fi-fo-fum," Brett said. "I'm about to huff and puff and blow you two cowardly fucks all the way down to hell."

Metal scraped against wood. The bathroom door jerked forward, smacking the open closet door, which held position. Then it started to jerk back, the opposite way it should have.

"Goddamn it," Brett muttered. "Missed one."

He pulled the door harder but whatever he'd forgotten to remove still held it firmly in place. There was a thump as something was knocked over and rattling as several metal objects rolled across the floor outside. Brett swore again and moved away from the bathroom to grab what he needed. *Toolbox*, Jack thought, swallowing his fear. *He's taking the door off its hinges.*

Taking Diane by the shoulders, Jack kissed her as hard as he could, their teeth clacking together. Blood flowed from one or both of their lips as they scraped in their frantic intensity. He released her and said, "Can you fit through that window?"

Diane stared at him uncomprehendingly for a moment, then looked over to where he was pointing.

"I think so, but Jack—"

You'll never make it, she clearly wanted to say.

Jack knew. He didn't care.

"Climb up onto the roof. Get into the access stairwell if you can, and if not, run around screaming your lungs out. Drop down onto someone else's balcony and bang on the window. Someone is bound to hear and call the police."

Before she could say *I'm not leaving you* he was dragging her toward the jacuzzi, lifting her by the waist and stepping up onto its rim so she could reach the bottom of the window. His burned chest muscles screamed in agony. Fresh blood and pus oozed from the cracked, burnt skin that had been his nipples. But Jack kept her steady. He remembered how the first time they made love he had picked her up from cowgirl position and walked her across their hotel room so he could fuck her against the wall, never once losing his grip on her or falling out, Diane crying out in surprise and pleasure. The memory gave him the strength to continue.

Ignoring the mess in the tub and trying not to slip, Jack nearly smacked Diane into the corner of the wall. She reached up and grabbed the top of the windowsill, pulling herself upward. Jack held onto her legs while she reached up and turned, her upper body vanishing from his sightline.

"I can see it! I can see the roof!"

She was sitting now, half-inside and half-outside.

The door to the bathroom rattled again.

"Go," Jack said. He dropped to one knee, his foot splashing in the blood bath, and choked back bile as he gave her the boost she needed. Her legs slipped out of the window and shot upward with the rest of her.

There was a resounding crash as the bathroom door finally came free from the wall. Jack didn't know how long it would take for the closet door to come down.

He swallowed his pain and his fear, climbed down from the jacuzzi, and punched one of the mirrors over the sink with his already damaged pinky-less right hand. The pain was negligible compared to the rest of what he had already suffered. The shards rained down. Jack grabbed the largest piece he saw, squeezed it in his palm. Ready to die fighting.

4:01 AM

THE WIND BLEW DIANE'S HAIR into her face as she ran barefoot across the rooftop. Despite the lights of the sleeping beach town, she could still see stars dappling the night sky. The cold ocean air reinvigorated her. It was as if the rest of the world were real again. After hours of enduring the terrors in the condo, reality returned with a vengeance.

She didn't have to go far. The door to the maintenance stairwell, somewhat unnecessarily labeled "Employees Only" and "No Trespassing," was less than ten feet from where she had climbed up. Diane grabbed the handle and tried to turn it, but it wouldn't budge. She saw the electronic lock and cried out in despair.

Jack was probably dead by now.

There would be no more sunrises or bike rides together. No more dinners, no more movies, no more lovemaking. They would never reminisce about their past or dream about their future again. Her escape attempt had achieved nothing, only ensured she would die alone in the fresh air with a beautiful view. Maybe Jack was right. There was no God, and if there was an omnipotent force controlling or observing her fate, it was cruel and merciless.

Diane sank to her knees and sobbed. Somewhere unseen a seagull began cawing, as if mocking her.

"Shut up!" Diane screamed. If she'd been wearing her shoes she might have thrown them into the void at her unseen tormentor. "Shut the hell up!"

"Jesus, calm down lady. What's your problem?"

Diane nearly fainted. She looked around for the source of the voice and saw nothing. It had sounded so close. She must have finally snapped. After everything she had suffered tonight it was a wonder it didn't happen sooner. She waited for the speaker to reveal themselves. When they didn't, she cried out again.

"Hello! Can you still hear me?"

"Yes," the voice said, impatient now. "Keep your fucking voice down. My dad just got my little brother back to sleep. You want him to the call the cops?"

Diane realized the voice was coming from the balcony next to Brett and Claire's unit. It was the voice of a teenage girl. She ran back the way she'd come, nearly flinging herself over the railing to lean down, trying to see her guardian angel. A cloud of candy scented vape floated up.

"Yes! Call the police! They're killing my boyfriend! They tried to kill me!"

The skeptical face of a teenage girl appeared. She looked up at Diane, perplexed.

"How did you get up on the roof?" the girl asked.

"Listen to me," Diane screamed. "The people in the condo next to yours, Brett and Claire Hinsey, tried to kill me and are about to kill my boyfriend. My name is Diane Prescott, and his name is Jack McKee. We're from Pittsburgh, Pennsylvania. We're staying at the Quality Inn on the boardwalk. If you don't call the police right fucking now, he's dead. Do you understand?"

"Dad!"

The girl disappeared from view. Diane heard muffled shouting. In a minute a groggy but familiar voice called up to her.

"Listen, if this is some bloody prank—"

"Dan, this is not a joke!" Diane said. "Brett and Claire said they're going to kill you and your wife and kids next. Call the fucking cops!"

Another voice joined Dan's below. A woman, sounding panicky and asking endless questions. A toddler began to wail. Beneath the chaos, Diane could make out the teenager's voice, trying to repeat the information she had given her to a 911 operator.

Got you bastards, Diane thought. *I got you. You're not getting out of this.*

Her moment of triumph ended as quickly as it began.

And neither is Jack.

The rest of her life flashed before her eyes: being rescued from the roof and taken to the hospital by paramedics; multiple interviews with police officers; hours of testimony in a packed courtroom; non-stop news coverage by ravenous media vultures; endless scrutiny and attention from anonymous internet sleuths; the possibility of Brett and Claire's eventual release twenty or thirty years from now, if they were even convicted; growing old and alone no matter what else might happen, never willing to love anyone again after losing Jack.

She heard Andrea's voice in her ear. It told her to give up. Accept it. Just lie down and take it or jump.

Diane walked away from the family's balcony and back toward Brett and Claire's. She leaned over the railing. They were a corner unit. She could see their balcony perfectly. Knew she could climb over and drop down onto it if she wanted to.

And that was exactly what she did.

Diane swung one leg over the rail, then the other, and pushed herself off, landing on all fours like a housecat.

The blinds were still open. She could see the bathroom door completely off its hinges, resting on the bed.

Gently, she tried the door. It was unlocked. She slid it open a crack and listened.

Diane heard Brett hammering away at the closet door, no doubt with one of his steroid bloated shoulders. Claire was cheering him on. Diane had anywhere from seconds to a minute left to act. Announcing her return from this way guaranteed death.

She moved to the balcony's railing, climbing over with her back facing the ocean. Her heels hung over empty air, and again Andrea's voice implored her to let go, fall back, give up. Diane adjusted her grip, took hold of two balusters, and kicked off.

She slid down faster than anticipated, palms burning as flesh was torn away. One false move and it was all over. She was hanging from the balcony. Her wrists were held in place by the horizontal rail support. *Don't look down,* she told herself. Instead of a wall, her toes were touching open space. She strained to lower herself further. Her back and shoulder muscles were being pushed to their limits.

The cool metal of a top rail met Diane's feet.

She took a deep breath, raised herself slightly as if about to begin a set of pull-ups, then swung herself forward and let go.

This time Diane's landing was far from perfect. She banged her tailbone on the balcony's railing and knocked over one of the deck chairs. Scrambling to her feet, she tripped and smacked her body against the glass door, fumbling for the handle. It was unlocked just like the one upstairs.

Stepping into the living room, where the night's horror began, should have been terrifying. Surreal. But instead of dread, Diane felt nothing, even as she heard the closet door upstairs being struck with increasing ferocity. She moved forward with a single-minded purpose.

Save Jack.

Her eyes passed over the scattered Monopoly board and money, the upturned couch, the crooked coffee table where Jack's severed fingertip still lay on the cutting board, the dry puddle of his blood and the broken zip ties.

She saw Jack's cigarettes and his lighter.

Diane grabbed the lighter, only meaning to hold it up to the smoke detector, get Brett and Claire back down here and away from Jack. She stepped into the kitchen and noticed amidst the clutter of dirty dishes on the countertop a spray can of air freshener.

4:06 AM

BREAKING THE CLOSET DOOR DOWN was more difficult than Brett had anticipated, but it only served to fuel his rage. He didn't even mind the splinters that now dappled his triceps. The Urge was in full throttle. Jack and Diane were both going to get it, dead or alive.

He stepped back to catch his breath and assess the damage. One more good hit should do. Brett licked his lips, checked that the Eagle's safety was off again and gave his erection a quick tug through his shorts. A drop of pre-cum bloomed through the fabric. Just as he was about to resume his assault, Claire put a hand on his sweat-soaked back.

"Do you hear something?" she asked.

Brett lowered his gun and listened carefully. He heard something alright.

Soft fluttering movement. Nearby.

He turned his head toward the sound, stepping away from the bathroom and toward the bed. It was closer now. Claire joined him, her brow furrowed.

"It sounds like—"

"The blinds," Brett said.

Their balcony door was opened maybe a quarter of an inch. Just enough for a breeze to come through. Brett could have sworn it had been shut all day. They never locked their balconies. There was no point, this high up.

He hurried over and closed it, but something else unnerved him. Before he closed it, he thought he could hear voices from another balcony. Who else would be awake this late, or rather, this early and outside? Before he could shake it off or change his mind and investigate, a piercing electronic shriek tore through the penthouse.

The smoke detector was going off.

"What the fuck is that about?" Brett asked.

"I don't know," Claire said. "Don't yell at me!"

He pushed past her and hurried downstairs, meaning to rip the thing out of the ceiling. He had no patience left. Not even for Claire. Taking the steps two at a time, Brett thought, *Stupid spoiled bitch probably left the stove on. Never had to work a day in her life. Always taking me for granted.*

He stopped halfway down. That was no way to think about his wife. None of this was her fault. He decided to apologize for his tone when he went back upstairs, promising himself to do something special for her to make up for it. If that meant putting in extra effort to be nice to her parents this weekend, then he would.

Brett reached the first floor and turned the corner.

Diane stepped out from the hallway.

He saw the lighter and the spray can, saw the orange flame flickering and her finger going down, saw his first taste of hell rapidly approaching and all he could think before the pain started was: *Claire.*

4:08 AM

SHE WAS TRYING TO LOOK into the narrow gap that had appeared between the closet door and the bathroom wall to determine what if any tricks their captives might try to pull, had already identified the water flowing all over the floor and was looking forward to warning Brett to watch out for it despite his unwarranted rudeness to her just now, when she heard the screaming.

For the first time in her life, the sound frightened rather than aroused Claire because she understood immediately who was making it and why.

Claire flew down the stairs, barely holding onto her knife and not thinking as she moved through the air. Her heart pounded and her mind was utterly blank as fear flooded her body.

She smelled Brett before she saw him.

He was in the kitchen, thrashing and flailing, beating at his own face and arms as fire licked through his skin and released thick black smoke. The sound that continued to come from his throat was choked, guttural, and dying. He knocked plates and cups piled along the counter to the floor in a panic, groping blindly with both hands for something.

The gun. Where's his gun? Claire thought, just before three unsilenced shots rang out.

One caught Brett in the stomach, and as he twisted in pain the others struck him in the back. He landed face down on the floor still burning, still groaning, still dying.

Claire stood immobilized, ears deafened by the bullets, eyes blinded by smoke and tears.

Then she saw Diane, impossibly standing there holding the gun in her trembling hands, the silencer on the ground at her feet. She hadn't noticed Claire yet, was too busy looking down at Brett with a look of utter contempt on her face. Claire didn't know how Diane got out of the upstairs bathroom. She didn't care. What did it matter?

Without Brett, there was nothing left to live for.

Claire watched as her arm raised the knife automatically, blade down, ready to end it all. She braced herself. *I'm coming baby,* she thought. Diane still hadn't seen her. Claire inhaled sharply through her nostrils, knew what she had to do.

She rushed forward.

No one was leaving this condo alive.

4:09 AM

"***YOU BITCH!***"

Diane whipped around, raising the gun, ready to fire, but it was too late.

Claire's knife caught her in the shoulder. She dropped the gun and was slammed back against the kitchen island. Spit flew from the blonde's lips as she snarled, her beautiful face contorted into hideous animalistic rage.

"*You killed my B!*"

The knife came free and was about to plunge downward again, this time aimed right at her heart. Diane caught Claire's wrist in both hands. Using her entire body weight, she thrust herself forward and forced Claire back toward the stairs, hoping to get on top of her.

Claire screamed and pushed back, grabbing hold of Diane's hair with her left hand and pulling as hard as she could. They spun around, both colliding with the wall. A photograph of a sailboat came loose from its nail and landed on the ground with a crash.

Both women held onto one another, neither daring to loosen their hold. Claire was trying to smash Diane's head against the wall. Twisting, Diane brought her right knee against Claire's side as hard as she could.

Claire let go of Diane's hair involuntarily, her left hand going to her bruised and probably fractured ribcage. Taking the opportunity, Diane swung Claire by the arm as hard as she could toward the glass table. She was strong, and the rich bitch couldn't have been more than a hundred pounds. Claire lost her footing and the knife, landing on top of the coffee table, which collapsed beneath her.

Diane moved back toward the kitchen, trying to find where the gun had gone, only taking her eyes off Claire for ten seconds.

It was all the time Claire needed.

She'd gotten up and thrown herself at Diane's back with surprising stamina, but in her haste neglected to grab her knife. Instead, she sunk her teeth into Diane's wounded shoulder and clawed at her face with her manicured nails.

Diane screamed, taking hold of Claire's arms in a desperate effort to protect her eyes. She spun around through the living room, trying to shake her off, ramming her into the wall, the dining room table, and the island counter. But Claire was like a mad dog, rabid, teeth sinking deeper until they were scraping Diane's collarbone. They slammed into the television, knocking it and the DVD collection onto the floor. Dizzy from pain and blood loss, Diane almost let go.

Then she caught sight of the ring on Claire's hand.

Not her gaudy wedding ring. The garnet ring. *My ring*, Diane thought. With renewed hate and fury, she opened her own mouth and bit Claire's fingers as hard as she could.

Claire howled as Diane's incisors ripped through nerves and separated the bones. They released one another, both collapsing onto the glass-covered floor, the other's blood pouring from their mouths as they coughed and sputtered.

Diane spit out two of Claire's fingers. From one she removed her ring. She sat up, glaring at Claire in defiance, and put it back on. Her back was to the couch. She scanned the ground for the knife, hoping to plunge it into one or both of Claire's crazed eyes. The hilt was poking out from beneath the TV.

Right next to Claire.

With an evil smile, Claire grabbed the knife and staggered to her feet. Her teeth were stained red. Her entire body was covered in cuts of varying depth. Standing in front of the open balcony, the wind blowing behind her, she looked like a deranged succubus who'd just crawled up from the depths of a BDSM-themed hell.

Diane tried to stand. She couldn't.

Claire laughed, a horrible high-pitched, broken, deranged laugh that made her earlier shrieks sound utterly sane by comparison.

"Bitch," she said. "I hope he was worth it."

Claire took a single step toward Diane.

The bullet hit her directly in the mouth.

Claire's teeth and jawbone exploded in a gush of red and white. She staggered back onto the balcony, dropping the knife for the last time as her chin split in half. From the hole that used to be her lower face a hideous wet sound erupted. Before Diane could begin to guess what if anything she could possibly be trying to say, Claire was outside going over the rail and then she was gone, plummeting to the hard ground below.

From the smoke-filled kitchen, Jack limped forward. He was paler than he'd been when Diane left him in the bathroom. But he was alive.

"You okay?" Jack asked.

"No," Diane said.

"Me neither."

He helped her stand. Supporting one another, they inched their way out of the living room and back to the kitchen. They covered their mouths with their shirts, found the fire extinguisher under the sink and drenched Brett's corpse with it, then searched his pockets until they found his keys. By the time they pried the last lock off the front door they heard sirens approaching from the open balcony. Jack let the gun fall from his hands on their way out.

They wouldn't need it anymore.

After all, they had each other.

ACKNOWLEDGEMENTS

Thank you, Mom and Dad, for all those summers on the boardwalk. Thank you, Carrie, for answering my question about the woods in Bel Air and your general Maryland wisdom. Thank you, Michael, for reading and making me rewrite the first chapter—I don't believe this would have been published without your feedback. And thank you to C.V. Hunt and the Grindhouse Press team for taking a chance on this story.

Steven Caumo grew up in Meadow Lands, Pennsylvania, and has a Master of Fine Arts in Creative Writing from the NEOMFA program.

Other Grindhouse Press Titles

#666__*Satanic Summer* by Andersen Prunty
#113__*The Landlord* by C.V. Hunt and Andersen Prunty
#112__*The Freakshow: Rebirth in Drayton Falls, Volume 2* by Bryan Smith
#111__*Drive-Thru of the Dead: Drayton Falls, Volume 1* by Bryan Smith
#110__*Inhospitable* by Ali Seay
#109__*Violência* by Sultan Z. White
#108__*From the Void* by Bryan Smith
#107__*Corpse Mountain* by Andersen Prunty
#106__*Depraved Halloween* by Bryan Smith
#105__*Dread Ink* by Bryan Smith
#104__*Jack and Mr. Grin* by Andersen Prunty
#103__*What Ever Happened to Jo Rose?* by Chris DiLeo
#102__*I Think I'm Alone Now* by Ali Seay
#101__*Cute Aggression* by Emily Lynn
#100__*Headless* by Scott Cole
#099__*The Killing Kind* by Bryan Smith
#098__*An Affinity for Formaldehyde* by Chloe Spencer
#097__*Kill The Hunter* by Bryan Smith
#096__*The Gauntlet* by Bryan Smith
#095__*Bad Movie Night* by Patrick Lacey
#094__*Hysteria: Lolly & Lady Vanity* by Ali Seay
#093__*The Prettiest Girl in the Grave* by Kristopher Triana
#092__*Dead End House* by Bryan Smith
#091__*Graffiti Tombs* by Matt Serafini
#090__*The Hands of Onan* by Chris DiLeo
#089__*Burning Down the Night* by Bryan Smith
#088__*Kill Hill Carnage* by Tim Meyer
#087__*Meat Photo* by C.V. Hunt and Andersen Prunty
#086__*Dreaditation* by Andersen Prunty
#085__*The Unseen II* by Bryan Smith
#084__*Waif* by Samantha Kolesnik
#083__*Racing with the Devil* by Bryan Smith
#082__*Bodies Wrapped in Plastic and Other Items of Interest* by Andersen Prunty
#081__*The Next Time You See Me I'll Probably Be Dead* by C.V. Hunt
#080__*The Unseen* by Bryan Smith
#079__*The Late Night Horror Show* by Bryan Smith
#078__*Birth of a Monster* by A.S. Coomer

#077__*Invitation to Death* by Bryan Smith
#076__*Paradise Club* by Tim Meyer
#075__*Mage of the Hellmouth* by John Wayne Comunale
#074__*The Rotting Within* by Matt Kurtz
#073__*Go Down Hard* by Ali Seay
#072__*Girl of Prey* by Pete Risley
#071__*Gone to See the River Man* by Kristopher Triana
#070__*Horrorama* edited by C.V. Hunt
#069__*Depraved 4* by Bryan Smith
#068__*Worst Laid Plans: An Anthology of Vacation Horror* edited by Samantha Kolesnik
#067__*Deathripping: Collected Horror Stories* by Andersen Prunty
#066__*Depraved* by Bryan Smith
#065__*Crazytimes* by Scott Cole
#064__*Blood Relations* by Kristopher Triana
#063__*The Perfectly Fine House* by Stephen Kozeniewski and Wile E. Young
#062__*Savage Mountain* by John Quick
#061__*Cocksucker* by Lucas Milliron
#060__*Luciferin* by J. Peter W.
#059__*The Fucking Zombie Apocalypse* by Bryan Smith
#058__*True Crime* by Samantha Kolesnik
#057__*The Cycle* by John Wayne Comunale
#056__*A Voice So Soft* by Patrick Lacey
#055__*Merciless* by Bryan Smith
#054__*The Long Shadows of October* by Kristopher Triana
#053__*House of Blood* by Bryan Smith
#052__*The Freakshow* by Bryan Smith
#051__*Dirty Rotten Hippies and Other Stories* by Bryan Smith
#050__*Rites of Extinction* by Matt Serafini
#049__*Saint Sadist* by Lucas Mangum
#048__*Neon Dies At Dawn* by Andersen Prunty
#047__*Halloween Fiend* by C.V. Hunt
#046__*Limbs: A Love Story* by Tim Meyer
#045__*As Seen On T.V.* by John Wayne Comunale
#044__*Where Stars Won't Shine* by Patrick Lacey
#043__*Kinfolk* by Matt Kurtz
#042__*Kill For Satan!* by Bryan Smith
#041__*Dead Stripper Storage* by Bryan Smith
#040__*Triple Axe* by Scott Cole

#039__*Scummer* by John Wayne Comunale
#038__*Cockblock* by C.V. Hunt
#037__*Irrationalia* by Andersen Prunty
#036__*Full Brutal* by Kristopher Triana
#666__*Satanic Summer* by Andersen Prunty
#035__*Office Mutant* by Pete Risley
#034__*Death Pacts and Left-Hand Paths* by John Wayne Comunale
#033__*Home Is Where the Horror Is* by C.V. Hunt
#032__*This Town Needs A Monster* by Andersen Prunty
#031__*The Fetishists* by A.S. Coomer
#030__*Ritualistic Human Sacrifice* by C.V. Hunt
#029__*The Atrocity Vendor* by Nick Cato
#028__*Burn Down the House and Everyone In It* by Zachary T. Owen
#027__*Misery and Death and Everything Depressing* by C.V. Hunt
#026__*Naked Friends* by Justin Grimbol
#025__*Ghost Chant* by Gina Ranalli
#024__*Hearers of the Constant Hum* by William Pauley III
#023__*Hell's Waiting Room* by C.V. Hunt
#022__*Creep House: Horror Stories* by Andersen Prunty
#021__*Other People's Shit* by C.V. Hunt
#020__*The Party Lords* by Justin Grimbol
#019__*Sociopaths In Love* by Andersen Prunty
#018__*The Last Porno Theater* by Nick Cato
#017__*Zombieville* by C.V. Hunt
#016__*Samurai Vs. Robo-Dick* by Steve Lowe
#015__*The Warm Glow of Happy Homes* by Andersen Prunty
#014__*How To Kill Yourself* by C.V. Hunt
#013__*Bury the Children in the Yard: Horror Stories* by Andersen Prunty
#012__*Return to Devil Town (Vampires in Devil Town Book Three)* by Wayne Hixon
#011__*Pray You Die Alone: Horror Stories* by Andersen Prunty
#010__*King of the Perverts* by Steve Lowe
#009__*Sunruined: Horror Stories* by Andersen Prunty
#008__*Bright Black Moon (Vampires in Devil Town Book Two)* by Wayne Hixon
#007__*Hi I'm a Social Disease: Horror Stories* by Andersen Prunty
#006__*A Life On Fire* by Chris Bowsman
#005__*The Sorrow King* by Andersen Prunty
#004__*The Brothers Crunk* by William Pauley III
#003__*The Horribles* by Nathaniel Lambert

#002__*Vampires in Devil Town* by Wayne Hixon
#001__*House of Fallen Trees* by Gina Ranalli
#000__*Morning is Dead* by Andersen Prunty

www.ingramcontent.com/pod-product-compliance
Lightning Source LLC
LaVergne TN
LVHW030922080826
845145LV00013B/3013

* 9 7 8 1 9 5 7 5 0 4 2 9 2 *